IN THE EYE
OF THE
BEHOLDER

CHARM CITY DARKNESS
BOOK 4

KELLY A. HARMON

Pole to Pole Publishing
Baltimore

PRAISE FOR STONED IN CHARM CITY

"The story is fast paced and kept me glued to the pages... I couldn't put this one down. I seriously can't wait for [the next book] especially after the ending that had my head spinning."

~ 5 Stars

"By far one of the best Urban Fantasy books I have read. Each chapter had me on the edge of my seat, waiting with anticipation for what would come next. "

~ 5 Stars

"Kelly Harmon is an amazing author. This story covers good and evil in a way I haven't read before."

~ 5 Stars

PRAISE FOR A FAVOR FOR A FIEND

"This book ROCKS. Fast paced, with smooth crisp writing, Kelly A. Harmon's characters leap off the page. I could see our heroine and her helpers as they went about their ways. I read it in one sitting, it was that good. I highly recommend this book."

~ 5 Stars

"This fast-paced story keeps you turning pages until the very end. I cannot wait for the next installment. Another 5 stars!"

~ 5 Stars

"Kelly Harmon has once again captured my heart and attention. This is the second book in the series and I am not disappointed."

~ 5 Stars

Other Stories by Kelly A. Harmon

Charm City Darkness Series:
Stoned in Charm City
A Favor for a Fiend
A Blue Collar Proposition

Blood Soup
Selk Skin Deep
On the Path
The Dragon's Clause
Sky Lit Bargains
To Live by the Sea
Lies

In The Eye of the Beholder

Published 2017 by Pole to Pole Publishing
Book and cover design copyright © 2017 by Pole to Pole Publishing.

Cover Designed by Rio Nugraha.

ISBN-13: 978-1-941559-21-5
ISBN-10: 1-941559-21-2

Library of Congress Control Number: 2017960303

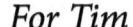

For Tim

IN THE EYE
OF THE
BEHOLDER

CHAPTER 1

The demon Pournelle materialized into Jo Byrne's Turning Wheel pagan shop after closing hours, as Jo was restocking the candles. He took a deep breath, savoring the heady, mixed odor of loose herbs and scented candles. A cone of strawberry incense burned in a brass dish near the door.

It must be her favorite, he thought, remembering the same scent was burning the last time he'd been here.

The flotilla of fairies with their tulle wings and feathered skirts—along with a dragon armada—hung still and silent from the ceiling. Since he hadn't entered through the door, no breeze moved them. A small radio played an old grunge tune softly somewhere near the cash register. He'd met the lead singer in Hell. Shame, that. The band could have made millions.

Pournelle pointed a finger at the bell on the door and waggled it. The bell rang as if a customer had just entered the shop.

WE'RE CLOSED," JO SAID, TURNING TO FACE THE latecomer. "I'm sorry. I thought I'd locked—" She felt the blood drain from her face, and she dropped the box of slender, white candles she'd been holding. They clattered to the floor, breaking the seal, and candles rolled in all directions. Heart thumping, she stood still and cursed herself for three kinds of fool for her deer-in-the-headlights reaction.

"It's not what you think," Pournelle said, holding up a hand. The starched, white cuff of his dress shirt was in direct contrast with the smooth, black skin of his forearm, and stuck out far enough for Jo to notice the black and silver cuff links.

She cleared her throat, and said, "I think there's a very powerful—uninvited—demon in my store."

"Well, if that's as far as you've gotten," Pournelle said, dryly, "you'd be right. But there's more to it than that, I'm afraid."

"I'm certain there is," Jo said, taking a step backward. She fingered the silver and malachite bangles on her wrist, wishing she had worn more protection. Black tourmaline would help, but Pournelle stood between her and the case with the gemstones. Her new rosemary bush sat next to the cash register—could she reach it in time if he chose to attack her? A few other things caught her eye—but none within easy reach. Jo inched toward the free-standing counter—and the rosemary.

"You have nothing to fear, I assure you," Pournelle said.

He remained standing where he was, so that encouraged her, but not much. "I'm not so certain of that."

The demon nodded, and a look that passed for sorrow flitted across his dark face and was gone.

Sorrow? Why did that make her want to hear more from him? Was this a trick?

"Why are you here?" she asked.

He smiled—*was that hope on his face?*—and snapped his fingers. The electric tea kettle Jo kept behind the front counter clicked on and started to warm the water inside. "We need to talk," he said. "Could you spare a cup of tea?"

POURNELLE KNEW HE HAD TO TAKE THIS SLOWLY. There were a half a dozen things in the store that Jo could use to send him straight back to Hell. One of them would send him back as an amorphous puddle of goo. He couldn't have that, even if he was trying to mend his ways.

Turning the other cheek only went so far in his book. He wouldn't turn it so far as to sacrifice himself. If he were willing to die for what he believed in, he could have done that a thousand times over in the last century. This was about living. And escaping Hell.

But first, he needed an ally. Or at least a friend. Someone who might be willing to help him, should he ask.

He'd start with someone who would listen. *Jo.*

Jo moved behind the front counter and switched off the radio. She pulled two mugs from beneath the glass case.

"Lapsang Souchong?" she asked.

He pulled a face. "Much too smoky. Do you mean to be insulting?" *That since I'm a creature of Hell, I must enjoy the taste of smoke? That's not the way it works.* He tsked. "I was hoping for *friendship* tea." He smiled to let her know he wasn't kidding. Jo laughed anyway.

"You have a lot of nerve asking for friendship tea, Mr. Demon—"

"Pournelle."

She nodded. "You have a lot of nerve, Mr. Pournelle."

"Just Pournelle." He smiled, hoping it looked more genuine than feral. "I would like to be your friend."

"Coming from any other guy, that statement would come off creepy, and maybe a little insane," Jo said. She rummaged below the cabinet, found a bright yellow cylindrical cardboard container way in the back, and plunked it onto the counter. She peeled off the plastic lid and peered inside. "You're just scary, but I think I'm holding it together pretty well. You've piqued my curiosity. I can only hope that doesn't get me killed."

Instant tea mix, Pournelle noticed. Crystalized into a single rocky lump. There was no way that stuff was coming out of the container.

Frowning, Jo grabbed the letter opener near the cash register and jammed it into the solidified crystals over and over again. Bean-sized pellets of instant tea broke off the main lump.

It was Pournelle's turn to frown. "You're not actually going to serve me *instant* tea?" he asked, a note of disdain in his voice. "Especially *that* instant tea." He frowned more. "Serving me instant tea might get you killed yet."

"You're the one who's kidding now, right?" she asked, sparing him a brief glance.

And as if she hadn't heard him, she spooned three teaspoons of rock-hard mix into each mug, poured boiling water over them, and stirred. *A lot.* Then she pushed a cup in his direction.

Their fingers brushed and Pournelle felt instantly drained—and more than a little nauseated. Jo was ill, and it wasn't just any illness—it was tainted with evil.

His own plans could wait. She needed his help.

"You really want me to drink this?" He asked, trying to buy a little time to think. Under normal circumstances, he would have been highly offended by the idea of instant tea and would have simply refused it. Oh, who was he kidding? He was still highly offended. But helping Jo trumped instant tea. He would help her, and maybe she would help him. That's what friends were for, right?

Jo looked up at him and smiled, the fake kind of smile you offer to unwanted guests and insulting mothers-in-law. "The polite thing for you to do would be to accept this cup, take a sip, and tell me how good it is. And then you can tell me why you're *really* here."

"But the *right* thing for me to do is to tell you how much I'll hate tasting that, let alone drinking it gone. Isn't that what friends do? Tell the unvarnished truth, even though it hurts? I've expressed my displeasure at the idea of drinking instant tea. How can you stand there smiling and still feel obliged to serve it to me?"

She sighed and sat down on her stool, appearing to consider what he said. Finally, she answered. "You're right in many ways, but that doesn't apply here. After all, I'm giving you what you asked for."

"Instant does not qualify as anything better than swill." He snapped his fingers.

In less than a trice, a tall, narrow samovar appeared at the end of the counter on a large silver platter. A hand-painted tea pot—small blue and orange flowers on the creamy China background—sat on top of it. Two matching porcelain tea cups, filled to their golden rims with steaming black tea, rested on the platter next to a silver dish of lemon slices. The tart, citrus aroma of lemon, freshly sliced, pervaded the strawberry scent of the shop. The fragrant odor of fresh tea wafted in Jo's direction. *One should always serve a friend her favorite tea using the best he had to offer,* Pournelle thought.

He smiled, reached for a cup, and placed it directly in front of Jo. "Tea, in friendship," he intoned.

She frowned—again—then turned her colorful, yellow tea canister to face him. The label read *Friendship Tea.*

She quirked an eyebrow at him. "But you asked for *friendship tea.* I gave it. *That's* what friends are for."

CHAPTER 2

JO WATCHED POURNELLE STARE AT THE TEA canister and the happy smile slide right off his face. Frankly, she'd been surprised she still had the stuff under the counter. Pournelle was right—as far as tea was concerned, it was an abomination. But it really *was* Friendship Tea. She'd received it as a Secret Santa gift at a Chamber of Commerce holiday party some years ago. The woman who'd given it to her told her she'd concocted it herself from a recipe she had found on the Internet.

It was tasty, as long as you didn't think of it as *tea*.

Pournelle snapped his fingers, looking suddenly contrite, and the samovar, the scent of fresh lemons and everything else he had conjured disappeared as quickly as it had come.

"You're absolutely right," he said, pulling the mug of *Friendship Tea* toward him. "I apologize."

The apology stunned Jo to the core.

He lifted the tea cup to his lips and sipped. Without making a face, he took a second, larger, sip, then sat the cup back down on the counter. "It's delicious," he said, staring into her eyes, apparently sincere.

Jo couldn't help herself. She burst out laughing. "Well done," she said, wiping tears from her eyes.

"I *am* trying," he said.

She took a sip of the tea herself.

He seemed to relax then, as if things would be okay. They'd shared something together.

"I do come in friendship," he said. "I'm here to warn you that your life's in danger."

And just like that, she was tense and wary again. She took a deep breath. "Your delivery needs some work," she said. "Friends try to break things to each other gently."

"I'm out of practice," he said, nodding. "It's been almost five hundred years since I've held a conversation in friendship. I'll try again."

She shifted on her stool, suddenly weary. She'd felt tired and achy a lot over the last week or so. She hoped she wasn't coming down with something.

Pournelle cleared his throat. "Would you like to move upstairs?"

"Excuse me?" He wanted to go to her apartment? Was he making some kind of demon move on her?

"You live above the store," Pournelle said. "Perhaps you would be more comfortable up there? I know I would be. These stools leave much to be desired in the realm of relaxation."

Jo shook her head. *Unbelievable,* she thought. But Pournelle said he came in friendship—which made her very, very curious—even if the delivered message was so ominous. "What the hell," she said, grabbing her mug. "Come along." She led him to the staircase she'd had built when she'd bought the apartment above the store. The original owner of the building had had it torn out when he'd rented the retail space below, but continued to live upstairs. He came and went via the outside fire escape. That had gotten old fast. So, once Jo had officially owned the apartment, she'd had the staircase built. She'd lost more than four feet of width from her store, but it was totally worth it to not have to go in and out of a window to the fire escape, and enter her own store via the front door.

She unlocked the door at the top of the stairs and they stepped into her private domain.

Two, low armless love seats faced each other on an area rug in front of a formstone fireplace. A low coffee table made of a simple glass plate over stacks of hardbound books rested between them. The hardwood floors gleamed.

A simple dining room followed in the open floor plan, and then came the kitchen—the only enclosed room on this level. On the left wall, another staircase led up.

Jo sat down on one of the love seats and gestured for Pournelle to sit across from her. "Now why don't you tell me what you want to say."

He nodded. "You know how certain demons in Hell always seem to be gunning for Assumpta?"

"Demetrious and his gang? They used to," Jo said. "It's been a few months since we've seen anything—not since Assumpta forced him back to Hell."

"Not Demetrious—"

"But—"

Pournelle raised a hand. "Demetrious was sent back to Hell in disgrace, his power halved. You won't have to worry about him ever again. But the rest of his lackeys are regrouping and jockeying for the position of leader of the Baltimore area." He sipped his tea. "And they're still gunning for Assumpta."

"Why? She's more than a simple threat to them. Demetrious isn't the only demon she's sent back to Hell. She's proven herself more than once. Why would they go up against her again?"

"Because she's also a *prize*. She has a strong faith in God. Her soul is *pure*. The demon who succeeds in dragging her into Hell for eternity will rise quickly in rank and power. So, there are rumblings of a new plan to capture her—"

"But her soul isn't as pure—" Jo stopped, afraid that she'd revealed too much.

"What do you mean?"

She shook her head. "It's not my place to say. Let's get back to your warning—"

Pournelle locked his pleading eyes with hers. "I can assure you that every word I say is true."

And Jo believed him, despite the fact that he was a demon. Despite knowing that demons inherently lie. For whatever reason, Pournelle wasn't lying to her right now. She'd bet her store on it. But what she didn't understand was his motivation. He wouldn't be telling her all of this if he were still a part of them—as he'd been in the past. Pournelle had done his fair share of menacing Assumpta. So why was he distancing himself from these demons now? Surely, that put him in a lot of danger. "You're not working with them," she said. It wasn't a question.

Pournelle shook his head. "Not anymore."

It was the opening she wanted. "Why not?"

POURNELLE DIDN'T KNOW HOW TO ANSWER. Would Jo believe anything that came out of his mouth? He'd never done anything to her, but he'd done plenty to Assumpta. And Jo and Assumpta were friends. He was lucky Jo was even talking to him right now.

"Let's save that story for another time," he said, sidestepping the issue.

He might have originally come here to admit just what she was asking him, but having learned that she was ill? *Unnaturally ill.* He was convinced her illness was related to what was going on in Hell with this new run at Assumpta. So, there was no question that he would help her. They had no time for his problems right now, only hers. "Time is of the essence," he said.

"Of course it is."

Pournelle gave her an inquisitive look. *What did she mean by that?* He said, "Look, I'm trying to impress upon you that the demons still want Assumpta. It's become a matter of honor with them. She's beaten them more than once, and they want their revenge. She always seems to have some power up her sleeve, some help from...*higher* authorities—" Pournelle stopped, thinking about what he'd just said about *power*. He wondered if the other rumor he'd heard was true. That it wasn't just about a pure soul and the desire to bring down a dangerous foe that had so many demons gunning for Assumpta. Did she possess something they all wanted? And if so, what did she have? "—they'll stop at nothing this time to get her," he finished.

Jo set her cup down on the coffee table. "Why aren't you telling her this?"

"Because it's *you* they're coming after."

She gasped. "Remember, friends break things to friends gently. If I hadn't already been sitting, I might have wilted to the floor."

Pournelle nodded. "I apologize."

"How did I become involved?"

"You're her friend. The demons figure if they can't get to Assumpta on her own, they'll get to her friends first. And you don't have her allies."

Jo ran a shaking hand through her spiky hair.

"What can I expect?"

I haven't the foggiest idea, Pournelle thought, cursing—again— his lowly status in Hell. If he were more connected, he'd have more answers.

"I don't know yet," he said. "Right now, everything is in the planning stage. Nothing's been decided except that they'll go after Assumpta's friends and family. After that, your guess is as good as mine. But when I do learn something concrete, I'll let you know. I figured you could take this time to plan, maybe set up some additional wards. Get more protection for yourself."

JO FOUND HERSELF NODDING—AGREEING WITH him. And feeling faint. She stood, and swayed on her feet. She reached for the back of the love seat to steady herself.

"I need to ask you to leave now," she said.

"You don't look well," Pournelle said, standing and reaching for her elbow. He steadied her.

"It's nothing. It'll pass," Jo said, knowing the lie for what it was. This faintness had been her steady companion for weeks now. It was only growing worse. She needed to see a doctor.

She took a deep breath, knowing she needed to take better care of herself. Knowing she needed her rest. "But you really must leave."

Pournelle nodded and dipped his hand into his inside breast pocket. He pulled out a small white box, about four inches square and half an inch thin. "This is for you."

"A lovely parting gift?"

"A token of friendship," he said. "Open it."

She did. An Egyptian scarab lay on a bed of white satin. She tucked the lid under the bottom of the box and lifted the beautiful metalwork. The pendant's burnished copper felt heavy in her hand; the wings inlaid with lapis lazuli made a striking contrast. Black beads, or polished stone, made up the eyes.

"It's beautiful."

"Wear it," Pournelle said.

With a snap of his fingers, he was gone.

CHAPTER 3

JO WOKE TO A BLAZING SUN AND THE FEELING
that she'd been hit by a Mack truck. Shards of piercing light,
reflected from the clear faceted pendulum hanging in the window,
bounced off the walls, adding to her discomfort. She groaned, sat up
in bed and put her feet on the hardwood floor. Dizziness struck her so
hard and so fast she almost collapsed back into the bed. She closed her
eyes and took a deep breath, willing away the vertigo.

She'd been feeling run down lately but nothing like this.

She stared at the scarab necklace resting on the night stand. The
beetle seemed to stare back at her from the tabletop.

Was the dizziness due to Pournelle? None of the reference texts
she'd read mentioned that being in the mere presence of a demon could
make one sick. Surely, she would have felt something last night? No.
Her sick feeling had nothing to do with his visit. She was just working
too hard, trying to build her business.

Or maybe, it was the scarab.

She took one more peek at the accusatory necklace and discounted
that idea. It wasn't making her sick...but it had to be *something*. Some
kind of spying device? A paranormal bug—*in the shape of a bug!*—
transmitting stuff to Pournelle? Maybe not that, but it couldn't be
nothing. Pournelle wasn't likely to simply give her a pretty bauble—
even in the name of friendship.

Rising on shaking legs, Jo made her way to the bathroom, listing slightly to the left all the way down the narrow hall. Her head was pounding. She splashed cold water on her face, ran wet hands through her spiky hair to tame the worst of it, and studied the bags under her eyes.

She'd slept like the dead. Why was she so tired now?

She opened the medicine cabinet and took out the thermometer, knowing she had a fever even before she checked. She just needed to know how bad it was. It would be a good barometer for how lousy her day was probably going to be.

One hundred and one point nine. Not great, but out of range of hallucinations. She could deal with that.

That's the bad thing about working for yourself, she thought. *No time off for good behavior.*

At least she had a short commute.

Jo took some aspirin, and then jumped into the shower. By ten-thirty a.m., she was downstairs in the shop and opening for the day, only a half an hour late.

She needed to finish replenishing the candles, drink a bracing pot of tea— maybe not in that order—and then give Assumpta a call. They had *much* to talk about.

CHAPTER 4

JO'S DAY HAD BEEN LOUSY, FULL OF CUSTOMER
returns and customer bitching. The dizziness had abated,
but her fever had spiked. She couldn't put off a visit to the doctor
any longer—and there'd been no time to call Assumpta. She'd call her
tomorrow, when she hoped to be feeling better.

With a heavy sigh and a growing desire to crawl back into bed
rather then walk the six blocks to the night clinic, Jo bundled up
warmly against the weather and left before she could talk herself out
of it.

The night was cool and helped her headache. She hurried, before
the feeling wore off.

The night clinic was packed.

Jo hated the place, but someone who worked for herself couldn't
just close shop mid-day and head off to a doctor appointment. So,
night clinic it was. She knew the place would be packed. It was *always*
packed. And tonight, it was stifling hot. She was already sweating
under her jacket.

She signed in at the front and took a seat on a hard, plastic chair
near the door where the air was likely to be cooler—and fresher. She
didn't relish the thought of breathing in the polluted air of the doctor's
office. The last thing she needed was to pick up an additional virus
while she was here.

She closed her eyes and leaned her head back, shutting things out while she waited for her turn.

The heat made Jo groggy, and she fell asleep. She knew she was dreaming, but she couldn't wake herself up.

*J*O PLODDED UP EASTERN AVENUE FROM THE *harbor, toward Highlandtown. Patterson Park was on her left across the street. She walked on the sidewalk in front of row homes, the handrails of their marble stoops decorated with lights and holly for Christmas. She dodged six-foot Santas and sleighs encroaching the walkway.*

It was cold outside, freezing, and the wind cut right through her coat, but she was burning up, her hot face an odd juxtaposition against the cold wind slapping her cheeks. Her legs and arms felt heavy, like she couldn't take another step. Yet, she continued walking at the same, slow speed, unable to stop. Although cars drove up and down the street at the pace allowed by the traffic lights, she couldn't hear them—she couldn't hear anything.

No—if she concentrated hard, she could hear all the usual sounds of the city—tires on the road, honking cars, a radio playing Latin music, someone speaking Polish, the slamming of the front door of Sharkey's Tavern, followed by uneven footsteps—all muffled, as though she were hearing it from under water.

Another block and she stopped at South Linwood Street for the traffic light. The Casimir Pulaski Monument, though set back from the street quite a way, loomed in her vision. There was something about it, something she needed to remember. She stared at it, willing the memory to come.

It hit her as the light changed. In front of the monument was a manhole cover leading to the sewers below Baltimore. No—the metallic cover disguised a portal to Hell—not sewers. She'd helped Assumpta ward it against The Big Guy, the most powerful demon in the Mid-Atlantic area. Maybe that's where she needed to be. In the sewers—in Hell.

The light changed again. Now she'd have to wait for it to cycle in order to cross to the park.

Cars swarmed from the left, from the Inner Harbor, some of them wet, as if they'd just passed through a storm. The more cars that passed, the wetter they looked. Water streamed off their bumpers, wetting the road. More wet cars passed, these with their windshield wipers whipping at full speed, water sluicing from them and running into the street, rolling down Eastern Avenue.

More water careened down the road, chasing the cars, getting deeper, bringing the scent of the harbor with it: dead fish, too long in the sun; boat fuel; salt air. Soon the cars disappeared, replaced by the swiftly moving water, now rising over the sidewalk.

The light changed again, but Jo couldn't cross. The water was too swift, too deep, relentlessly driving up Eastern Avenue toward Highlandtown.

Beyond the rising river, on the paved ground of the park in front of the Pulaski Monument, Jo watched the manhole cover rise a few inches and slide across the pavement, exposing the gate of Hell.

Three figures climbed out of the hole. One poked another and then pointed at her, laughing. The other joined in. The third waved his hands in her direction, and she felt searing pain on her arms.

She looked down to see her arms sleeved in black tattoos: skulls and snakes, dancing skeletons, tiny spiders, all hidden in intricate designs from shoulder to wrist. She felt the same pricking, the same pain on her stomach, and bent over, heaving. She vomited dark harbor water—her mouth full of the taste of oil slick, dead fish and salt.

MS. BYRNE?"

The voice barely penetrated Jo's dream.

"Ms. Byrne!"

"Huh!" Startled, she stood up, still tasting salty brine in her mouth and smelling the diesel and fish odors of the harbor. Her stomach trembled, and she hoped she could keep from vomiting here.

The nurse told Jo she could follow her to the back.

Jo followed the nurse, thinking about the dream. The first part she got, the steady plodding and confusion—it was all related to being ill. And water signifies the unconscious self. She was feeling overwhelmed. *True.* But the figures, demons most definitely, since they'd climbed out of the manhole she knew to be a portal to Hell—what did they mean?

"Symptoms?" the nurse was asking as she gestured for Jo to step onto a scale in a hallway alcove.

"I'm really tired, even when I get enough rest. Some muscle pain, a fever that comes and goes..." She shrugged. "But the worst is the dizziness..." Jo explained how it came and went at the oddest times. She probably sounded like an infomercial for the symptoms of the latest fad pill, but she'd been over this enough times in her own mind that it all spilled out in a torrent. The nurse touched a stylus to various points on the tablet she carried.

"Any chance you could be pregnant?"

"Not a one," said Jo. Another tap of the stylus.

"This way," the nurse said, leading Jo to the second room on the left. "Sit here." She gestured to a paper-covered table. "Take off your sweater please."

Jo sat, opened her mouth wide when the nurse shoved the thermometer in her face, and gave her arm when the nurse brought a blood-pressure cuff. She tried not to grimace when the nurse pumped it up too hard.

"Low," the nurse murmured, putting the cuff away and jotting on the tablet again. The thermometer beeped. She took the probe from Jo's mouth, expertly ejecting the plastic sleeve into the trash can, and looked at the meter. "High," she said, looking at Jo for the first time with some concern. "Are you experiencing any dizziness now?"

"No. I feel like my head is going to cave in." She rubbed her brow, trying to alleviate the pain. "And I'm really tired, like I've already said."

The nurse made a notation on her chart and walked to the door. "The doctor will be with you in a minute."

"Hurry back," Jo said softly to the retreating nurse. She had the urge to lie down on the paper-covered table, but wasn't certain she would get back up again if she did.

Eventually, she did lie back on the paper. She didn't care if she fell asleep. She needed a nap. Might as well take one here as on the couch when she got home—except that she couldn't sleep because it felt weird in the doctor's office on this narrow examination table; she could hear people talking in the hallway and the incessant ticking of the clock on the wall.

So, she waited, counting ceiling tiles and floor tiles, and refraining from opening the cabinets.

The doctor came in just when she'd given up hope of seeing him. He was in his forties, she guessed from his receding hairline and soft belly, and he looked tired, but not as tired as she felt. His dark hair was rumpled, and he kept a pocket protector in the left pocket of his sparkling-white doctor's jacket.

"Sorry I've kept you," he said, looking at the tablet in his hand, "Jo." He made eye contact and smiled. "Why don't you tell me what's wrong?"

She explained her symptoms again while he pressed his fingers to the glands in her neck and then listened to her breath.

He laid a cool hand on her brow. "I think we need more tests. I'd call this flu, but you don't have any cold symptoms. Let's see what your blood says."

She closed her eyes and nodded, resigned to putting up with this for a few more days. "Can you do that here, or do I have to go elsewhere for the tests?" She didn't think she had the energy to find one of those testing places tonight.

"You're in luck. We've got a phlebotomist on staff. She'll take your blood, but we'll have to send it out to find out what's wrong. It will be somewhere between twelve and twenty-four hours before we know anything. In the meantime—"

"Get some rest and drink plenty of fluids?" Jo asked.

The doctor smiled. "Absolutely. We'll call you with the results and either have you come back in or just call in a prescription for you."

He held out his hand and Jo shook it.

"Can I take aspirin for the headache?"

"Certainly."

"Thanks, Doc," she said.

He nodded and left the room, letting her pull on her sweater in private.

She made her way up the hallway, gave a check to the receptionist, and left.

The night air cooled her face again, lending her a bit of much-needed energy.

The city sounds were different at night, fewer car horns, less traffic. And the air was sweeter with less exhaust from commuters. The six-block walk home was more comfortable than her walk to the clinic, even in the semi-darkness of the streetlights.

About halfway to home, Jo heard footsteps behind her. She picked up the pace, clutching her handbag to her waist. *You just never knew in the city*, she thought. She'd never been mugged, and she didn't want tonight to be the first time. The sound of the footsteps grew louder. Her heart raced.

Calm down, she told herself. It might be someone in a hurry to get home, like her.

Still, she couldn't help increasing her speed, her heels hitting the pavement with louder *claps*. She didn't want to be overtaken.

"Jo," said a man behind her.

She stopped and turned, her heart still beating rapidly but slowing. Her eyes widened.

"Pournelle." She took a deep breath, relaxed the stranglehold she had on the strap of her purse. "You scared me."

"I'm sorry," he said, stopping beside her. His suit jacket was open, revealing a subtle paisley-patterned vest beneath. His wingtip shoes gleamed from a high polish. "I thought perhaps catching up to you like a human rather than popping up next to you like a demon, would be less troublesome." He cleared his throat and buttoned his suit jacket, as if girding himself for battle. "You're not wearing the necklace," he said.

"It's pretty, but it doesn't go with this sweater." *And I don't know what it does, so I'm not wearing it,* she thought.

"You should wear it all the time. Even if no one sees it."

Jo gave Pournelle a studied look. It was important to him that she wear it, so giving it to her was definitely more than a friendly gesture. *Yep, it was magical.* She narrowed her eyes at him. "Why do you want me to wear it?"

"It will protect you," he said, glancing away from her.

But the way he said it made her uncertain. He was hiding something. What could it be? She couldn't ask him—couldn't let him know she was suspicious. What if it *were* dangerous and her prying made him angry? He was demon, after all. What would he do to her in anger? She'd seen his temper. Could she actually trust that he wanted to be friends?

"I'll put it on when I get home tonight," she said, knowing she would do no such thing. But it seemed easiest to placate him. Maybe he would leave her alone after this.

"Good," he said, reaching into his hip pocket and pulling out a plain, white business card. He offered it to her, and she automatically took it. "Call me if you need me," he said. With a snap of his fingers, he was gone.

Bewildered, Jo stood there a moment staring at the card, her thumb caressing the thick, rich paper, while she silently read his name written out in fine, gold calligraphy.

He was a demon, but he'd given her his name. He was placing his trust in her—but *why?*

CHAPTER 5

JO WOKE WITH THE SAME LETHARGY AND
dizziness she'd felt the night before. Getting upright took
some effort. She made a pot of tea, took a long hot shower, ate some
aspirin—along with her toast—and made it downstairs to open the
shop on time.

She set her phone, the white box containing the scarab necklace
and Pournelle's calling card on the counter, and flicked on a few lights.
Then, she took a deep breath, willing herself to feel better. The day
awaited, and she needed to get past whatever it was that was making
her so feel so awful.

But first she needed to cleanse the shop, dispel some negative
energy and bolster protection. She'd skipped her morning and evening
sage-burning routine a couple of times in the last two weeks since she'd
felt so ill. But not anymore. If Pournelle was right, she couldn't afford to.

Jo reached for her sage and a lighter, and started the ritual in
the back. She closed her eyes, mentally preparing herself and focusing
on the intent of pushing out negative energy, cleansing the store and
protecting herself and her customers. Then she opened her eyes and
lit the tightly bundled herb. As it smoked, she walked the perimeter
of the store, paying special attention to the corners and doorways,
wafting the smoke more heavily in these areas and making certain to

trace the outline of the doors. She also cleansed the area around the front counter and cash register—where negative energies always seem to accumulate—before finishing with extra care at the store entrance. She extinguished the sage.

Jo watched dust motes dance in the beam of sunshine streaming in through the glass of the front door while she unlocked the deadbolts and flipped the *Closed* sign to *Open*. She lit a cone of strawberry incense, breathing deeply of the sweet scent while she placed it on a high shelf near the entrance, then she turned on the rest of the lights.

Behind the counter, she turned the radio on softly to the local rock station and picked up her new phone to text Assumpta—glad she'd convinced her friend that a phone was a good business investment. Now, they had a steady means of communication for times like this.

Normally, she'd call, but today she just didn't feel like it. *How bad was that?* She texted Assumpta.

[Morning! Need your help. Come over later?]

Jo laid the phone by the cash register and took her electric tea kettle into a small bathroom and filled it with water from the sink. She set it to boil, prepared some loose tea in a porcelain pot, and found her favorite mug among several under the counter. The mug was black with the word ATTITUDE written in tall, hot-pink letters all the way around the mug.

She wasn't feeling much attitude this morning. She hoped the mug would instill some.

Her phone buzzed.

[Hung over. Sunday night?]

Jo's spirits sank. She'd forgotten Assumpta was out of town for her cousin Sheila's wedding. Yeah, she could wait, but she didn't want to. She wanted answers about the necklace *now*. She texted back.

[Absolutely. Have been gifted with a beautiful necklace from Pournelle I want you to look at.]

Jo snapped a photo of the scarab in its box and sent it along after the text. Her phone dinged back almost instantly.

[See you soon!]

Assumpta's reply appeared mere seconds after the image finished sending. *Soon.* What did that mean? Soon compared to what? Assumpta wasn't due back until the day after tomorrow. That would have to be soon enough.

She sighed and picked up her favorite tarot deck with Norse artwork in stunning colors. It was the deck that got her through high school and college—even though she was horrible at divination. They had a soothing energy which never failed to calm her, as they were doing now. Jo smiled, grateful for small blessings.

She shuffled the deck and laid out a yes/no spread, planning to ask whether or not the necklace was harmful. But she changed her mind before turning the cards. She'd rather wait for Assumpta and her pendulum than act on faulty answers.

But she could do research and have some ideas before Assumpta got home. The scarab had to have some power, judging by Pournelle's insistence she wear it. *Maybe I can narrow down what kind of power,* she thought, sweeping up the tarot cards and setting them aside.

She grabbed her stepstool, then pulled a book down from her special collection on a sturdy shelf she'd had built over the large plate-glass window behind the counter. It kept the books out of the damaging sun and within handy reach when she wanted one.

The books contained knowledge of witchcraft, paganism, all kinds of religions, folklore and mythology, herbalism, the occult, and more. These were old and trusted tomes that she turned to often—the

Internet was no substitute for the kind of deep research she did, though maybe someday, she hoped. Her collection even contained a few spell books and diaries she'd found in second-hand stores and estate sales. Most were old, and at one end of the shelf sat her own book, a three-ring binder containing her current interests, favorite spells that she hadn't committed to memory yet, snippets of interesting conversation she'd heard from customers, and all kinds of research.

She pulled that down, turned to the back to find blank loose-leaf paper and wrote *Scarabs* in her bold script across the top of the first page. She underlined it, then underlined it again, then opened the first book and started reading. If she couldn't find what she wanted from her *top shelf* books, she'd head to the overflow in the storeroom—which was becoming a serious problem. Soon, she might have to give thought to dedicating some space to her *library.*

The doctor from the clinic called. Blood tests revealed nothing, so she probably did have a touch of the flu. Come back if it became worse. But thanks to Pournelle, she had a much better idea of what was happening. So, she wouldn't be headed back to the clinic anytime soon.

Customers came and went. She sold candles and herbs—her best sellers—one of the fairies hanging from the ceiling, and her most expensive athame. She'd been so elated she could have kissed the customer who bought it. The knife had been in the store far too long, and she was afraid she was going to have to reduce the price to sell it. The inventory roster showed it had been on the books longer than two years.

Note to self, she thought, *buy pretty items of* reasonable *retail value.* She needed to turn things over more quickly to keep her profits up.

She closed the book she'd been reading and rubbed her eyes. Nothing new in this one. Scarabs were representations of dung beetles—*which is kind of disgusting*, she thought, until she read more. The female dung beetle wrapped her new eggs in dung balls and then rolled them underground where they would be safe until born. Others in the **scarabaeidae** family rolled the dung balls into sunshine to warm them, encouraging it to hatch the next generation. *Who knew beetles had a mothering instinct?*

Scarabs were revered as protection talismans and were worn often. Sometimes their protections were dedicated: protection from harm, protection from financial issues, protection from loss, and more.

Could the scarab that Pournelle had given her be charged with some specific protection? He seemed concerned that she wasn't wearing it, particularly after he'd given her a warning that she was in danger. Perhaps it was a simple protection from harm.

Harm. The demons were out to get Assumpta's friends.

She felt a cold shiver run through her. She was in danger.

She needed to re-ward the shop—immediately. And her new apartment upstairs—with something stronger than her usual sage. Why hadn't she taken care of that sooner?

Because I'm feeling like crap, she thought, running a hand across her forehead. The worry hit her like ton of bricks; weariness came over her like a blanket of fog.

And because she'd been distracted by the scarab.

She took it out of the box, convinced by the scanty research she'd done that it wasn't going to harm her. Pournelle had offered her something of protection. Was he really interested in being her friend? Or was he trying to lull her into a false sense of security? Eventually, she'd find out, she knew. For now, she'd run with the assumption that since scarabs seemed to be inherently good, wearing hers could do her no harm. And, in fact, it would probably help.

She caressed a lapis wing with a fingertip, enjoying the cool, smooth surface of the gemstone. Then, taking a deep breath, she lifted the beetle by its delicate chain and placed it over her head. The scarab rested just above the laces of her peasant shirt, the copper warming to the touch of her skin.

She let out the deep breath, smiling. Did she feel better? Safer? She did. And she didn't care if it was some kind of placebo effect. She felt better—slightly better—than she had in days. She decided she wasn't going to dismiss it as some kind of mind game. As far as she was concerned, Pournelle had given her a powerful gift. It was already doing its job.

She closed the book and her binder and put them back on the shelf, making room on the counter top to do some magic. Even if she had a protective scarab, she needed additional wards, and she needed them fast. Something strong and powerful—something she could use to buy herself more time, because she knew she couldn't avoid the demons forever.

Her shop had once been exorcised by a priest—Father Tony— Assumpta's personal confessor. Jo shook her head. She'd never understood the Catholic way of having an intermediary between you and your god. Assumpta knew first-hand that Father Tony was no longer necessary for that, but he'd been a friend of Assumpta's family for such a long time. And Assumpta had once told her it was hard to quit confession cold turkey.

And though he was a die-hard Catholic, Father Tony had had no qualms about stepping into her *very* pagan shop, performing an exorcism, and then doing some major blessing. His price? A polite invitation to church, which she had just as politely declined. She liked that he stuck with his convictions but was open-minded enough to give her help.

Maybe Father Tony would come and bless the shop again. She'd had some major construction. There were new doorways to bless. She'd give him a call. She would put up with his lecture to come to Mass, but leave him little hope. She was an avowed pagan. He knew that, but it didn't stop him from trying the few times she'd seen him. But he didn't understand why a pagan might want her shop blessed.

He couldn't wrap his head around the idea that she perceived his prayer just as powerful as her spells. And besides, she'd seen it work. That's all the convincing she needed. There was just something about the rest of the Christian trappings that made her wary.

She placed a heavy black altar cloth on the counter and grabbed a basket from the store entrance, mentally counting the entrances and exits to her store and home, and then *went shopping* for what she needed. Rosemary, red pepper, paprika and other herbs, long white taper candles, small squares of burlap and colored twine, and myriad other items.

There were three windows and a door leading into the shop downstairs. Two windows were small, but one was the large storefront—she'd have to be extra diligent with that one—use some extra wards, making it clear that the portal was barred, so to be speak.

Jo had cleansed the counter with sage earlier, but still took the time to close her eyes and imagine a clean, protected space in which to work her magic. For good measure, she cast salt about the work area before she laid out seven squares of burlap, then lined each of them with a square of tightly woven cotton. In the center of the cotton, she placed the warding herbs of basil and mugwort, which protect against negative magic. She added blessed salt—which Assumpta had given her—pepper and paprika all to ward off magical attacks. Finally, she added protective elements—rosemary for personal protection; hematite, which protects home and property; and black tourmaline which provides protection on many different levels: spiritual, emotional, physical and mental, and for that reason is considered the most powerful protective element of all.

She picked up the four corners of the first charm to create a pocket, and tied it firmly with both white and purple twine—for additional physical and spiritual protection—and to keep everything in.

She'd finished tying off the second charm when, without warning, a good looking, thirty-something guy stood at the counter in front of her. She shrieked and stepped backward, smelling the tell-tale odor of sulfur. A demon.

Intricate black tattoos sleeved his arms from his wrists to as high as Jo could see beneath the black T-shirt he wore. *Skulls and snakes, dancing skeletons, and tiny spiders were all hidden in the lacy designs. Jo gasped. "You were in my dream—"*

"Are you sure it was a dream?" He laughed, then looked down at the counter and hissed. "Looks like I got here just in the nick of time." He rested his fingers on the cloth—just the tips of his fingers—as though he were preparing to type—and grinned. Smoke curled toward the ceiling, then little flames licked upward to his knuckles. He lifted his hands, and blew. Fire engulfed all of the cloth and herbs in one huge conflagration.

The fireball blasted upward, singeing Jo's face, and then disappeared.

"That takes care of that," he said, dusting his hands together. "Now let's take care of you."

In a blink, he was behind the counter with Jo, his hands on her shoulders, squeezing painfully, pushing her up against the wall next to the plate glass window.

"Don't kill me," she blurted, immediately angry with herself. She'd never considered herself the begging type.

"You flatter me—but I wouldn't *dream* of it, sweetheart," he said, breathing his sulfurous breath in her face. "I'm only here to deliver you a warning. Besides, it wouldn't do at all to kill you the first time I'm ordered to stop by. Where's the fun in that?"

Claws sprang from the tips of his fingers. She felt them, before she looked down to see them. Talons, several inches long, black and puckered, like bones charred over a fire. *This was going to hurt.*

She lashed out with her foot, striking his ankle.

He grunted but only held her tighter. "That little trick is going to cost you."

She choked on the hot, sulfurous breath streaming past her face. His claws squeezed tighter, pressing against her ribs. He clamped one hand over her mouth, wrapped the other arm tight around her waist, and leaned against her, pressing her into the wall. She couldn't breathe deeply enough. His bony claws pained her rib cage. If he held her any tighter, she wouldn't be able to breathe at all.

She struggled to get out of his grip, but it felt like trying to move through rock. Suddenly, her knees buckled and Jo sagged against the smooth wall, only the demon holding her up. *Dammit!* Why did the weakness have to come upon her now? She opened her mouth to scream, and the demon's hand covered it.

"I wouldn't do that, if I were you," he said. "Things will only get worse."

He uncovered her mouth, slowly.

Wondering if I'll scream anyway? she thought.

His eyes glittered with malice.

If only she could have called Pournelle, but she didn't have his calling card handy. She had tried memorizing his full name earlier, but it wouldn't stick. She could look at the card and know his name, turn it over—and in those few milliseconds—she'd already forgotten it. Apparently, the card was bespelled, preventing the reader from remembering his name.

She looked around for something to attack with, stretching her arm painfully toward the cash register's pencil cup, where she kept her letter opener. It wasn't sharp, but it didn't need to be to stab through something. But she couldn't reach it.

The demon dragged her up, his claws digging painfully into her stomach. One hand snaked across her chest, bumping the scarab.

"What's this?" he growled, clasping the metal beetle and holding it up to his face. Then he laughed. "Beetles for protection, eh? Not this one." The demon grasped the delicate chain, wrapping it around two fingers and preparing to yank it from her neck, but Jo grabbed the scarab, holding it tightly in her fist.

"No!"

The bell rang over the door and a customer walked in. The demon pointed at the young woman and she froze.

"We'll finish this later," the demon growled at Jo. "Tell Assumpta we know she's got the medallion. Unless she gives it up, we'll tear through all her friends and family—every last one of them—and then yours, before finally coming for her." He gave her a wry smile. "If she gives up the medallion sooner rather than later, we'll give her a little time to say goodbye to everyone before she joins us in Hell."

The demon disappeared. Jo stumbled on shaking legs the few feet to the counter and leaned against it, catching her breath.

Shaking all over, Jo smiled at the customer who was moving freely again, then sank down onto her stool. "Let me know if there's anything I can help you with."

The customer nodded and veered toward the candles and incense.

The medallion, Jo thought—a fist-sized amulet on a heavy chain that allowed the wearer to command demons and to see a demon's true form. Assumpta had told her she wasn't certain if the medallion contained the life force of a demon or if the necklace itself *was* the demon. Either way, it was powerful and probably could be used to do so much more than they knew.

Jo had thought only a demon known as Demetrious knew of the medallion—but maybe when Assumpta had banished back to Hell, he'd used the knowledge as a bargaining chip. Or maybe some other demons had forced him to reveal information. She'd never know. But she did know that those demons vying for the Baltimore seat of power knew Assumpta had it—and they wanted it back.

She had to tell Assumpta when she got back into town.

CHAPTER 6

A FEW HOURS LATER, THE SHOP'S DOOR SWUNG open and Assumpta rushed in. Her wavy auburn hair was windswept, the long curls tangled. She looked anxious.

If only she knew, Jo thought, sinking to a stool behind the register. Her legs couldn't hold her any longer. She was shaking all over—inside and out.

"You couldn't have picked a better time to walk through that door," Jo said, "but I thought you weren't due back until day after tomorrow."

"I wasn't," Assumpta said, "but when I saw your photo, I came running. How can you be so calm when a demon gives you a gift?" She sniffed. "And why does it smell like a fire in here?" She swung her voluminous purse up and set it on the glass-topped counter. "Knock over a candle?"

"One question at a time." Jo stood on still shaky legs, filled the electric tea kettle with fresh water and flipped the switch. She sat down again. "Pull up a stool. I'll tell you all about my demon visits."

"Pournelle?"

"And then some."

"This doesn't sound good." Assumpta dragged the second stool around to the back of the counter and sat near Jo. She moved her purse to the floor by her feet. "What's going on? And what's with Pournelle giving you gifts?" Assumpta raised an eyebrow.

"You're not suggesting he's coming on to me!"

Assumpta giggled. "I'm not suggesting anything. Just teasing."

"*I'd* go to Mass and say confession before getting amorous with a demon," Jo said. *Even one I'm beginning to understand—if not actually like.* That gave her pause. She dallied under the counter, considering it for a moment, before finding two clean mugs from the stash she kept there, and finally said, "Pournelle's visit was fairly innocuous. It was the *other* one I'm worried about."

"The other one?"

"Yeah." Jo described him.

"It doesn't sound like any of the demons that I've clashed with before," Assumpta said. "But that doesn't mean anything. There's got to be as many demons in Hell as there are stars in the sky."

"Exactly." Jo scrambled for a tin of tea.

Assumpta leaned forward and ran a finger over the glass. "This is soot. What are you not telling me?" She stood and headed for the small, private bathroom to the left of the counter. "Do you have some paper towels back here? Some glass cleaner?"

"Leave it," Jo said from beneath the counter, and then, suddenly overcome, stood, so she could sit back down on the stool. "I'll get it after we've talked." She was still too jittery to handle it now, and she couldn't let Assumpta clean up her mess. It wouldn't be right. She'd do it herself. But if she tried to do it now, she might just drop the cleaner through the glass and cost herself a thousand dollars she didn't have for a new display case.

"If you're sure," Assumpta said, not looking sure. "I'd really like to help."

"I'm sure. You can help dig out everything we need for tea."

Assumpta returned to the counter and rummaged below, pulling out a jar of loose tea labeled *orange-lemon citrus*, some paper napkins, sugar and some spoons. "Tell me about this new demon."

Jo sighed. "I get the feeling he was only a messenger—not really involved in all the intrigue—though he certainly took pleasure in his task." She rubbed her face, depositing a small bit of soot on her cheek. Assumpta handed her a napkin and mimed wiping it off. Jo grimaced and wiped the soot away. "In fact, his message was almost the same as something Pournelle said—only this demon mentioned the medallion, and Pournelle did not." She took a deep breath and felt a sharp pain in her ribs. She rubbed at it.

"What's that?" Assumpta asked, eyes wide. "Did he hurt you?"

"Not so much. Annoyed me. Pissed me off. Scared me to death," she said more softly, looking at Assumpta. "But not so much hurt me that I need any help on that front. At least not yet." She pulled up her shirt a few inches to reveal a slightly tanned stomach marred with red scratches where the demon's claws had scraped and the beginnings of five bruised spots, one for each claw on the demon's hand. She hadn't really expected it to look so bad.

"He did hurt you!"

Jo grimaced, running a finger down one of the scratches. Her belly muscles tensed from the pain. "Only scratches and bruises, really. Look, it didn't even draw blood. Trust me, it could have been much worse."

"It will be purple and black by tonight," Assumpta said. "I'm sorry."

Jo looked up from the bruising. "What are you sorry for? You didn't do this."

"If I had never walked into your shop, you wouldn't be involved. The demons wouldn't be coming after you. You wouldn't have any bruises or scratching. You wouldn't have been threatened."

"You don't know that." Jo pulled her shirt down, gently smoothing the gauzy material. "But I do know that things happen for a reason. This was meant to happen—we just have to figure out why."

"You sound like my grandmother."

Jo smiled. "Then you know I'm right." The smile slid off her face. "You're not going to like what he said."

Assumpta spooned loose tea into a ceramic tea pot and poured hot water over it. A burst of lemon rose up with the steam. She sat back down on the stool and crossed her arms on her chest. "Okay—hit me with it. What was the demon's message?"

Jo told her. Assumpta slumped on her stool.

"So, they still want me. You know, that was the whole purpose of the demon mark—to drag me into Hell. I can't say I'm surprised. But, I can't give them the medallion," Assumpta whispered.

"I know."

"It would damn me forever." Her eyes teared up. Then she took a deep breath, blinking rapidly to erase the moisture. "Worse, it would unleash a lot of evil in our world. We can't let that happen."

"I know," Jo said again. But did she know? From a practical standpoint, it would be better to hand over the medallion and stop all this demon mischief in their lives. The world would always be full of evil they would have to contend with. It might be easier to let the medallion go, and let this bit of threatening evil go along with it. But maybe that was the illness talking—she was so damned tired she didn't feel like fighting.

She reached for the steaming pot of tea and poured them both a full mug. Lemon still dominated, but now that the leaves had steeped for a few moments, she could smell the orange. She reached for some honey under the counter that Assumpta hadn't thought to grab, squirted a liberal dollop into her mug and stirred.

Assumpta continued in the same flat voice, "I should have handed it over to Saint Michael the moment he asked for it. I don't know what I was thinking."

Jo had a pretty good idea of what Assumpta might have been thinking, though Assumpta might not want to admit it right now: that even though she'd gotten rid of her demon mark, Assumpta had feared that things weren't over as far as demons were concerned. Keeping the medallion was like having an ace up her sleeve. And now that she had a moment to breath, all that Catholic guilt came rushing back at her. The guilt that said, *yeah, you should have given the medallion to Saint Michael, and since you didn't, you're headed straight to Hell.*

But from own perspective, the medallion was simply a tool, one which despite its origin—and with the right intent—could be used to accomplish so many good things. At the very least, it could be used as a bargaining chip. It would be a shame to give it away—to the demons *or* Saint Michael—just because they'd asked.

But that's not what Assumpta needed to hear.

"What do I do, Jo? I can't give it to the demons, but now I can't *not* give it to the demons."

Jo blew across the top of her tea and sipped before she answered. "There's always another way. We'll do some protection spells for your friends and family. That should buy us some time to figure it out." She handed Assumpta a pad of paper and a pen. "Make a list of all your family and friends."

"Now?"

"Now. There's no time to lose. Make the list. And when you're done, we'll need your holy water."

Jo got a beeswax candle and a small porcelain cauldron about the size of a grapefruit from the store shelves. She rummaged under the counter for a box of straight pins, and then settled everything on the glass countertop. While Assumpta wrote, she cleaned up the errant soot, feeling less shaky now that she had a purpose to distract her. Then, she retrieved her sage and cleansed the area again, wafting smoke all around the register and Assumpta.

Assumpta put down her pencil.

Jo asked, "How many people are on your list, including you?"

"Seventeen." Assumpta rummaged through her purse and set an opaque, plastic squeeze bottle on the counter. Her holy water.

Jo pushed the cauldron to the center of the counter and stood the beeswax candle onto a small white dessert plate. Three red rings were painted around the edge, one inside the other. She said, "Strip seventeen leaves from the rosemary bush and put them in the cauldron. While you're doing so, focus on keeping each and every one of your family and friends safe. Think about creating a fence or shield or barrier—whatever it is that you think is strongest—encircling each of them and keeping them from harm."

Assumpta plucked the leaves from the rosemary bush. "What words should I say?"

"Words are mostly irrelevant. It's your intent that matters. But if speaking words—or saying them silently—will help you focus better, then do it. Just speak from your heart." She pushed the candle in front of the cauldron, directly across from Assumpta. Assumpta nodded and closed her eyes. Her parted lips moved as she spoke silently. When she opened her eyes, Jo said, "Now pour the holy water over the rosemary—just enough to cover them all. And light this candle. Continue focusing on the protection of your family."

Assumpta focused on the candle, and after a moment asked, "Why the holy water?"

"We could have used any water, but I thought if you used the holy water it would make the spell more your own—and more powerful for you. We're almost done." She opened the box of straight pins and plucked out seventeen with white pearly beads on top. White for protection, just like the rosemary. "Pull a leaf out of the water and name it for one person on your list. Curl it into a circle and push a straight pin through it to keep it that way. Place that leaf on the dish around the candle. Do this for each leaf, making certain that the leaves form a circle around the candle when you're done—"

"Circles, within circles, within circles," Assumpta murmured.

"Exactly—encircling and protecting," Jo said. "Finally, focus on the flame, imagine its light traveling outward, pushing that protection toward your friends and family. When you've pushed all the energy you can into the flame, extinguish it. The spell is done."

Assumpta focused on the flame, and the air in the shop grew still. A few moments later, she leaned forward and blew out the candle. She let out a long, deep breath. "I'm tired."

Jo smiled. "As you should be. You've used your energy to protect your family."

"But will it be enough?" Assumpta gave her a plaintive look.

"Father Tony can help, if you'd like. He can pray. We'll spread as much protection around as we can until we can find an alternative."

"I could give myself up," Assumpta said, clutching her mug of tea close to her chest.

"And that would accomplish what?"

Assumpta shrugged and sipped from her mug. "Buy us some time, maybe."

"Having you is part of their end game. I don't think that will buy us any time." Jo stirred her tea. She changed the subject. "How did you know about Pournelle's visit? I was fairly certain I was being cool about it in the texts—no matter how *uncool* I was feeling."

"You *were* cool, but I noticed his calling card on the counter in your pic."

Making a face, Jo set the mug down, pulled out her phone and looked at the photo she'd snapped. There it was, Pournelle's card lying right beside the jewelry box. "Damn. I didn't even realize I'd left that there."

"May I see the scarab?"

Jo pulled the pendant out from under her shirt, lifted the chain over her neck, and handed it to Assumpta.

"It's stunning," Assumpta said, rubbing the thin chain between her thumb and forefinger. "And this chain is so thin it hardly feels like it will hold the scarab." She caught Jo's eye. "But are you sure you should be wearing it?" She handed it back. "Why would Pournelle give you such a beautiful thing?"

Jo shook her head. "I wasn't sure if I should wear it at first, but—" The bell over the front door rang and a middle-aged woman came in. She smiled at Jo and waved. Jo waved back, recognizing her as a regular, then continued her conversation with Assumpta in hushed tones. "—when I read that they're normally used for protection, I decided the risk was worth it." She shrugged. "And yet, it came from a demon. It really *is* gorgeous. But how do I know if it's evil or not? And does it matter if it's evil if it's used in a good way?"

Assumpta gave her a wry smile. "You're the one who's always telling me that intention is key, but I'm still struggling with that one."

"Because of the medallion," Jo said. It didn't take a genius to know that much. And with Caroline's death, and Sheila's wedding, she and Assumpta hadn't really had a moment to discuss it. And they might not have another chance until after Caroline's funeral. "Do you want to talk about it?"

"I used it," Assumpta said. Jo nodded, she knew that much. "I used it more than once—first to get rid of the demon mark, which was actually *another demon,* and then again to send Demetrious back to Hell." Jo hadn't known that. Assumpta took a deep breath. She looked like she was holding back tears. "I used it even though Saint Michael told me not to—even though he asked me to hand it over so he could destroy it. He said each time I used it, I put a black mark on my soul. And if my soul gets too black, I'm damned to Hell—" And there was the kicker, Jo thought. Assumpta continued, "—but how many times is too many times? And did talking with the medallion count as using it?"

"You talked with the medallion?" Jo sat her mug down on the counter. "How is that possible?"

Assumpta shrugged. "I don't know. I talked with it to learn how to use it. But I was never able to figure it out. Maybe there's a demon inside the medallion, or the medallion is possessed. For all I know, the medallion *is* a demon—just like the demon mark. I asked it, but the medallion would never admit what it was. My intent was good, Jo. So why am I still on the road to perdition?"

Before Jo could formulate a response, Assumpta sucked in a watery breath and wiped at her teary eyes. "But I didn't come here to argue theology or the consequences of one's actions," she said. "I'm here for you, and that gorgeous scarab necklace." She found a tissue and wiped her nose. "Let's find out if it's evil." Assumpta reached into her pocket and pulled out her pendulum, uncoiling the gold string and straightening it between a pinched thumb and forefinger. The inverted, teardrop crystal at the bottom of the string gleamed in the light. "First, we'll see if we can get a good reading."

Jo nodded. She lifted the tea pot to Assumpta in silent invitation. When she nodded, Jo filled both their mugs again.

Assumpta lifted the pendulum so it would swing freely and asked, "Am I visiting The Turning Wheel?"

Almost imperceptibly, the pendulum twitched at the end of its string. It began a slight to-and-fro motion, and then, gathering momentum, started to circle to the right.

"Clockwise," said Assumpta, smiling.

"So, it answered correctly," Jo said. "The spirits are with us."

Assumpta nodded. "Now, the double-check. Did Jo just ask me if I wanted a cup of coffee?"

This time, the pendulum made an obvious hitch at the end of its string, foiling its clockwise motion and swinging a-kilter. After a moment, it settled into a counter-clockwise spin.

"Conditions are perfect to obtain answers," Assumpta said.

"So, what is it?" Jo asked. "Is the scarab safe to wear? And why would Pournelle, of all people, gift me with it?"

From her purse, Assumpta pulled a crumpled piece of loose-leaf paper folded in half. The letters of the alphabet were written on the page in a semi-circle, A on the left and Z on the right, with L and M, hitting the high point of the arc. She smoothed it out on her lap.

"I'm not certain we can find the answer to the last question, Jo. That may be something only Pournelle himself can tell you. But the first two, I think we've got a pretty good shot at answering."

Assumpta lifted the pendulum and held it over the lettered paper. "Is the scarab necklace, which the demon Pournelle gave Jo, evil?"

The pendulum started it's back and forth motion, tiny little sways to and fro until it built up momentum. Then, the briefest hint of a counter-clockwise circle. Assumpta continued holding the pendulum aloft, letting the circle grow wider and wider, confirming the negative answer.

"It's not evil," Assumpta said. "I'm surprised."

"Me, too." Jo spooned honey into her mug and stirred her tea. "I don't understand why he would help me. He's a demon. Demon *equals* evil. Right?" Assumpta opened her mouth to reply, but Jo continued. "And yet, there was something about my earlier conversation with him that makes me think Pournelle, *despite* being a demon, is trying to do the *right* thing."

"The *right* thing?" Assumpta murmured, almost absently. A frown furrowed her brow. She laid the pendulum in her lap and pulled her tea nearer. After adding sugar, she blew across the top of the cup and took a sip. "Did Pournelle use those words? *The right thing?*"

"No." Jo gave Assumpta a hard look. *What was going on?* "Why do you ask?"

Assumpta drew in a deep breath. "We struck a little bargain, Pournelle and I."

Jo's eyes widened. "You made a bargain with Pournelle? Are you insane?" The last was nearly shouted.

Assumpta smiled ruefully, holding up her hands as if to stave off Jo's words. "Not really a bargain. Nothing signed on either side— no demon mark imparted. Just an understanding of *good will.* I think Pournelle is extending it to you."

"He actually went for that?" Jo gulped her tea. "I knew you were going to propose it to him, but when you didn't mention it again, I thought nothing had come of it. But *why* would he agree to that? And why include me in the deal?" She set her mug down on the counter. "But if he is including me, it explains the odd conversation we had before he gave me the scarab."

Assumpta gave her a questioning look.

"He told me that he'd come to me *in friendship.*"

"In friendship?"

Jo nodded and told her all that transpired—including serving Pournelle the dreadful *Friendship Tea.* They both laughed. Then Jo took a deep breath, shaking her head slowly. "I've got nothing to trade him for his friendship *or* his good will. And he's done me two favors already. I've offered him none. What's in it for him?"

Assumpta explained that good will doesn't require anything in return. "That's why I could offer good will to Pournelle, and he could do the same, and yet it's not a binding deal. What is given is not given with the idea that something else must be exchanged in consideration. It's not tit-for-tat."

"And since there's no deal, he can help you—or vice versa—and you don't acquire a demon mark on your soul. But that still doesn't explain why he's helping me."

"Maybe Pournelle's doing this because he doesn't want to alienate my friends. He wants to include them."

Jo shook her head, her expression serious. "He wants something from me."

Assumpta made a face at her. "I don't believe that. Good will comes with no strings attached."

"No demon makes that kind of deal."

"It's not a deal," Assumpta insisted.

"Maybe it's not a deal in the conventional sense, but it's a deal nonetheless. There may be no strings attached at the onset, but there's an implied promise that something is in the offing later down the road."

"But there's no obligation!" Assumpta slammed her fist down on the counter.

"You don't think so?" Did Assumpta actually believe that? Maybe she just hadn't thought it through. Jo said, "It's a logical conclusion. What happens if Pournelle does you favor after favor—getting you so deep in his *good will* debt, that when he does ask you for something, you'll feel obligated to help. And how much do you want to bet, that with him being a demon, the request will be something abominable?"

The question stretched between them for a few beats of Jo's heart.

"Do you really believe that?" Assumpta asked.

"I'm not certain." Jo wriggled on the stool, trying to find a more comfortable position. But was it the chair, or her conscience, that was uncomfortable?

Assumpta's voice was soft and low, almost sad in timber. "It really goes against my grain to put trust—even a tiny amount of trust—in a demon. And yet, I've seen Pournelle perform good will. I'm still not certain I could completely trust him, but I believe his acts of good will are genuine."

The shop bell rang again, and the middle-aged woman left with a cheery wave. Jo flushed. She'd been so deep in conversation she hadn't remembered her customer. The woman might have been standing at the counter ready to purchase something and Jo might have ignored her. She bowed her head, the last bits of steam rising up from her mug to warm her face. Then she straightened and lifted the cup, finishing the tea in one large swallow. "Let's get back to the scarab."

She told Assumpta about Pournelle's second visit. "He told me the amulet is some kind of protection. He insisted I wear it." A rueful expression crossed her face. "But I don't know what it protects me against. Can your pendulum tell us what kind of protection it might offer?"

Assumpta held the pendulum over the crumpled paper again and smoothed the string. "Does the scarab protect the wearer?"

The crystal teardrop twisted at the end of the string and swayed slightly, gaining momentum. A moment later, it started a clockwise spin. Assumpta continued to hold the pendulum. The longer she held it, the wider the pendulum spun. "Does the scarab need to be worn to provide protection?"

The pendulum continued to turn clockwise. After a moment, Assumpta shrugged and dropped it into her lap. "Well, you need to wear it in order to have its protection." She finished her tea. "Since it's not evil, no harm should come from wearing it. And if Pournelle and my pendulum are correct, it will protect you."

Jo fingered the piece, still unsure. "From demons?"

Assumpta gave her a sharp look. She lifted the pendulum again. "I suspect not. Why would Pournelle give you a weapon against him?"

"It's not a weapon."

"Trust me. In the right circumstances, something even as passive as protection can still be a weapon. Remember my holy medals?"

Jo nodded. "But they're blessed. That's why they burn any demon they touch. The blessing is the weapon."

Assumpta nodded. "I hadn't considered that. Maybe I need to put that to the test." She grinned. "Do you think your new, helpful Pournelle would let me test an unblessed medal against his demonic flesh?" Before Jo could answer, Assumpta lifted the pendulum over the lettered paper and asked, "Does the scarab protect against demons?"

The pendulum began its gentle swing to and fro, to and fro, finally picking up momentum. It spun counter-clockwise.

"No," Jo whispered. So, she had no protection against demons.

Assumpta coiled up the pendulum and put it back in her pocket along with the crumpled, loose-leaf paper. She wiped her finger along the edge of the counter, apparently looking for more soot. "Now, tell me about the fire here, and why you *really* think Pournelle is sniffing around. If he didn't give you protection against demons, from what does he think you need protection?"

CHAPTER 7

WHY DOES POURNELLE THINK I NEED protection? Jo thought. *It makes the gift of the scarab even more curious.*

The large, plate glass window in the front of The Turning Wheel rattled as a furniture truck rumbled down the street in front of the shop. Jo put a hand to her temple and rubbed. She was getting a headache, and she really didn't feel like talking about this anymore. She was grateful for Assumpta's help, her company. Usually. But right now, she felt like closing up shop, taking some aspirin, and crawling back into bed.

Maybe more tea would help. She started the electric tea kettle heating water again and rummaged for a different blend. "I don't know why Pournelle thinks I need protection." Jo shrugged, feeling helpless—and that made her angry. She wasn't a helpless person. It had to be the fatigue messing with her. "Pournelle said demons were going to come after me, and he gave me a scarab for protection. I just put two and two together and assumed the scarab would protect me against the demons. But it didn't...and your pendulum confirms it. But now...?" Her voice trailed off. "I haven't the faintest idea what the scarab is meant to be used for."

Assumpta gave her a look that was as forlorn as she felt. "You know, when I got rid of the demon mark, I *really* hoped we would be done with demons. I had no idea they'd formulate a plan to get to me by threatening my family and my friends." She flexed her shoulders, remembering the itch and pain of the mark—which had looked like a small bullseye, tattooed between her shoulder blades. "I can't believe Demetrios was such an *upstanding* leader that he inspired loyalty among his followers. Is that even possible—loyalty among demons?" She picked up the empty tea pot and rinsed it in the bathroom. Then, she spooned the new tea Jo had chosen into the bottom.

The kettle clicked off, and Jo poured boiling water into the pot. The citrusy scent of orange and black tea tickled her nose. "Maybe it's not so much a matter of loyalty as it is about losing a meal ticket. They thought they were going to have a free ride under his direction, but now it's all gone away, and it's *your* fault, Assumpta."

"It's not my fault!"

Jo smiled wryly. "Sure it is—you sent Demetrious back to Hell. But I wasn't serious about things being your fault. I meant that as an explanation of demon motivation: they blame you for their bad luck. But the more I think about that, the more I don't believe it. Demons don't bond over shared misfortune. They lie and backstab and grapple their way to the top, every demon for itself." She raised a hand to rub a sudden ache in the back of her neck. "I don't think we're up against a huge contingent here, maybe two or three separate demons—" She remembered her dream, and the three demons who'd clambered out of the manhole in front of the Casimir Pulaski monument. She told Assumpta what she'd dreamt. "The more I consider it, the more I'm positive we're up against a single demon with a couple of lackeys— or maybe one or two different demons, each desiring to take over Demetrious' place. With Demetrious back in Hell, the Baltimore area is without demon leadership. Eventually, one of them will rise to the top."

Assumpta was nodding. "That makes sense. I've really only ever been up against a single powerful demon. Most recently, I tangled with Demetrious. But when I was first demon-marked, I fought a single, nameless demon at Holy Rosary Church. Then came The Big Guy—

Caroline's beau, Adrian." Assumpta drew in another deep breath, clearly trying to hold back tears for her deceased friend.

"I'm so sorry about Caroline," Jo said. "If there's anything I can do…"

Assumpta nodded, and then she got angry. "Caroline isn't even buried yet! Whoever it is isn't wasting any time."

"Trying to get to you when you're at your lowest." Jo poured the fresh tea into hers and Assumpta's mugs.

"How are we supposed to figure out who's behind this?" Assumpta asked.

"I haven't the faintest idea—"

"I do," a deep voice said.

Assumpta nearly fell off her chair when Pournelle suddenly appeared beside her. "Don't do that!" she said.

"I really need to get this place better warded," Jo said.

"Time was of the essence," Pournelle said. "I overheard that someone was planning to get to you today, and I came as soon as I heard." He sniffed the air in the store and looked around, searching. "Fire? I see I didn't get here soon enough. Are you okay, Jo? Was anyone hurt?" He looked at Assumpta, and then back to Jo.

"I'm fine," Jo said. "*We're* fine. Assumpta wasn't here when I had my little demon visit."

"You're not wearing the scarab."

"I was showing it to Assumpta."

"Put it on."

Jo wasn't feeling very strong, but she wasn't going to let a demon order around. "I don't see why I should have to wear your gift. It's not like we're dating or anything."

Pournelle rolled his eyes. "I didn't give you the scarab because I *like* you. I gave it to you because you need it. You're really sick."

Jo gasped. "How did you know that?"

"What?" Assumpta said, looking to Jo. "You didn't tell me you were sick. What's wrong?"

Pournelle snapped his fingers and a tall, padded stool appeared. He sat and casually leaned an elbow on the counter. He spoke quietly, all of his attention focused on Jo. "I knew you were sick from almost the minute I first came to see you. When you made me tea, our fingers touched as you handed me the mug. I could feel the sickness in you then—it was quite apparent."

While he spoke, Jo found another clean mug under the counter, spooned in sugar, and poured the fresh tea on top. Leaving the spoon in the mug, she pushed it toward Pournelle.

He pulled the mug closer toward him and stirred. Pournelle said, "I could do nothing less than offer you a token of protection. Hence, the scarab."

Jo lifted the scarab by the impossibly delicate chain and placed it back around her neck. Was the protection supposed to make her feel better? If so, it wasn't working. Though perhaps she felt a bit lighter? It was hard to tell. Maybe she simply felt hopeful. "Then, I should thank you," Jo said. She blew out a deep breath and braced herself for the answer to her next question. "So, I'm sick. *Really* sick—how sick?" Her heart thumped in her chest. She needed to know the answer, but didn't want to know the answer if it were really that bad. She mentally calculated how much it was going to cost her to close up shop for a few weeks and get over whatever plagued her.

Pournelle's smile disappeared. "You're not just sick, Jo. You're dying."

CHAPTER 8

"DYING!" ASSUMPTA SHOUTED. SHE TURNED AN incredulous face to Pournelle. "Dying how?"

"Demonic necrosis," Pournelle said quietly.

"Dying?" Jo sat her mug on the counter with deliberate precision and straightened up in the chair. No wonder she'd been feeling so poorly of late. "What the hell is demonic necrosis?"

Pournelle looked away. He seemed embarrassed to say.

But what was he embarrassed about? How other demons acted? Does he think I consider him "one of them" now? Really?

He fussed with an onyx cufflink. "It's a wasting disease, starting at the cellular level, causing only mild discomfort at first. Dizziness. Nausea. Fatigue. But as more cells in the body die off, the pain begins—then worsens, as all of your organs start to fail and your body begins to shut down."

"But what does it target?" Assumpta asked, standing and wrapping her arms around Jo, hugging her tightly. "Maybe we can take some preventative measures..."

"It doesn't target any one thing," Pournelle said. "It targets everything. It's a slow degeneration of all parts of the body, causing maximum damage and maximum pain. It's subtle in the beginning, but designed to be obvious enough to reveal itself as a curse as the disease progresses."

No wonder the doctor couldn't find anything wrong with her other than the symptoms, Jo thought. He didn't know what he was looking for. And he would have never looked for cellular wasting *caused by demons.* "How long do I have?"

Assumpta gave Jo a final squeeze, then stepped to the side to get a better look at Jo. "You just learned that you're dying by some evil, magical means, and all you're worried about is how much time you have left?" She slapped her palm down on the glass top of the counter, startling both Jo *and* Pournelle. "How about, 'who did this to me?' Or, 'can I reverse this spell?' Don't just sit there and take it!"

"You're right," Jo said as a single tear leaked out of her eye and ran down her face. "I just assumed that if a demon was sitting here in front of me telling me I'm dying by some demonic means, then there's nothing to be done." She smiled and straightened up on her stool. "But give me a little credit. I'll be fighting mad in an hour. Once I take it all in." She turned to Pournelle. "Can you help?"

Pournelle cleared his throat. "I've already done what I can. I've given you the scarab. Wear it. Whatever you do, don't take it off."

Jo lifted a shaking hand to touch the scarab hanging by its impossibly delicate chain. She didn't know if it was a trick of her tired—shocked—mind, but when she felt the weight of the heavy, colorful beetle, she felt a little better. Lighter.

"This will protect me?"

"It will keep you alive, as long as you never take it off."

CHAPTER 9

THE NEXT MORNING, JO FELT TIRED AGAIN. HEAVY. Lethargic. She'd sunk down into a low funk without the bolstering spirits of her friends—friend and demon acquaintance? *No*, she had to count Pournelle among her friends. He'd gone against his own kind and offered her protection. That counted for something. He was a friend.

So she could only blame the fatigue on her feelings, since the scarab seemed to be doing its job otherwise.

On the other hand, Pournelle had only said the scarab would keep her alive. He didn't say it would take away the symptoms. Maybe she'd just have to live with the fatigue. And if that's all she had to contend with, she'd count herself lucky.

But she had work to do, so she dragged herself out of bed early and called Holy Rosary Church, leaving a message for Father Tony asking for his assistance. She'd have to put up with his request that she come to mass, but she could honestly tell him for once that she just didn't feel like it. He couldn't bully her to church if she were feeling unwell. That brought a smile to her face. Once he left, she'd open the shop and ward it to the hilt in between waiting on customers.

She completed her morning sage ritual, and then opened for business, lighting her usual strawberry incense once she'd opened the door.

Father Tony arrived a short time later, warding satchel in hand. It contained everything he needed to bless the store and her apartment upstairs: his stole—the long purple scarf he wore around his neck when performing religious duties—his exorcism prayer book, and blessed salt, holy water and chrism. These were the tools he needed to fight demons, protect people from evil, and bless her shop. She wondered what else he kept inside the leather bag.

She didn't stand when he approached the counter—the weariness again. She hoped she could get a handle on it soon. She hated feeling so weak.

Father Tony set his bag on the counter. "Hello, Jo. I have to admit, I was a little surprised you called and asked me to come back to the shop."

"I've said it before, Father, I'm a pragmatist. I'll take my help wherever I can get it." She stood up, put her elbows on the counter and leaned toward him. "I'll follow up with my own set of wards, but I'll let you lay the groundwork. I've seen it in action."

Father Tony gave her a shrewd look. "Why do you feel such a need for my services?"

Jo hadn't thought he'd delve this deep. She figured he'd take the opportunity to bless the shop and rattle her cage again to come to mass. She hadn't been prepared for his intuition. "I've heard it on good authority, that I need to protect myself. Since I spend my days in the shop and my evenings above it, I figured I needed to increase my spiritual protection."

"Whose authority?" He pushed back the clasp on the top of the bag and pulled the bag open.

"I'd rather keep that information to myself." Pournelle and Father Tony had clashed in the past—and he had some very strong opinions on the demon. What priest wouldn't? But she didn't need a lecture from the priest this morning on the friends she kept. What he didn't know wouldn't hurt him—or annoy her.

"You don't think your magic is strong enough to handle whatever it is you think is coming at you?"

Jo smiled, knowing he was baiting her.

"Didn't I mention my pragmatism, Father? I've got every reason to believe I have the skill to keep the beasts at bay, but I won't turn down help from any quarter—no matter what my spiritual beliefs."

"Are you saying you don't believe in *Him?*"

"Oh, no!" Jo's eyes twinkled. She enjoyed the banter. "I've seen the proof of His work, seen it work through *you*. You and Assumpta have made a believer of me—"

"Then come to Church! If only to give your thanks for *His* help."

That stymied her. She thought church was for worship. She hadn't thought to enter that solemn space to offer thanks for help received— particularly when she could, she presumed, simply offer it up from where she stood. Why did she need to go to a church?

"I can honestly say I'm not feeling well enough to do that today," Jo said, sitting back down. "Another time, perhaps? I really do appreciate you coming."

He nodded, peering more closely at her. "You do look a bit tired today. And I'll take a rain check on church. You know I'm always available to help anyone who asks." Father Tony delved into his satchel and pulled out his purple stole. He kissed it, and hung it around his neck, the long ends fluttering down to his ankles. Reaching into the bag again, he retrieved a plastic bottle of holy water, a glass jar full of blessed salt, and a much, much smaller bottle which held holy chrism—oil blessed by a bishop—setting each on the counter in a line.

"Shall we start at the back again?"

The last time Father Tony had blessed the shop, Jo had had an infestation of demonic *shades*—dark, shadowy creatures similar to ghosts. Although they hadn't actually harmed things, they'd scared away her customers. It had been terrible for business. While her charms were slow to work on the problem, Father Tony was able to quickly force them from the store, starting in the back and driving them forward and out the front.

"Upstairs," Jo said, nodding to the stairs. "With the new staircase inside the store, the space is all connected now."

He was nodding even as she spoke, snapping his satchel closed and lifting it from the counter. "And you don't have to enter and exit via a window and the fire escape. How unexciting." He grinned, the dimple in his left cheek appearing, making him seem younger than his forty-five or so years. He gestured to the stairs. "After you."

"Trust me, I find the staircase pleasantly normal. But if you don't need me, I'll just stay here and mind the shop."

"If you're sure, then."

"Absolutely. I trust you up there." She handed him the key to her apartment, which she kept locked during business hours. She kept the space chained off, but one never knew if someone—or some*thing*—dared to slip past while she helped a customer.

"I'll start in the back when I'm done upstairs," Father Tony said, taking the key.

"Perfect." Jo pressed the button on her electric tea-kettle, thinking that a cup of tea might boost her energy levels this morning. "I'll be waiting here." *Because I don't have the energy to go up and down the stairs right now.* "Tea?"

"Maybe when I'm finished." Father Tony went up the stairs, re-fastening the chain behind him before he walked up.

Not a single customer entered the shop for the forty minutes Father Tony was upstairs. Jo was torn between wondering where her usual early-morning business was and thankful that she could just sit and enjoy her tea—though it wasn't making her feel any better. And when Father Tony finally came downstairs, she felt a strong urge to ask him to come back later—but she knew it wouldn't be prudent.

"Do you think we could hurry things along, Father?"

He grinned. "Having a priest in the shop is bad for business?"

She hadn't even considered that. "Not at all. I'm just still feeling tired and thought I might close the shop for an early lunch and take a little nap."

"I'll see what I can do." He grabbed the vial of chrism and walked to the rear of the shop, to a window on the back wall, newly revealed.

Father Tony himself had helped tear down the shelves and plywood that had once covered it over.

According to the previous owner of the store, a small grocery at the time, merchandise frequently disappeared from the shop before he'd boarded up the window. Although Jo missed the display space, she loved the natural light it brought to the back of the store—even with the bars she'd been sensible enough to install on the outside of the building. It was a more elegant solution to deterring thieves. And having access to the portal enabled her to ward it, something she hadn't been able to do when it was boarded up.

Father Tony stuck his thumb into the open vial of chrism and upturned the bottle. When the pad of his thumb was coated with oil, he removed it, righting the vial, then drew an unbreaking line of oil around the window frame, re-coating his thumb when the oil grew too thin to create a barrier. When he was done, he used the chrism to draw lines around the large, plate-glass window in the front of the store, and then the front door, the only other entrances on the ground floor.

He walked to the counter. "Do you mind if I cut a few sprigs of rosemary?"

Jo handed him scissors from the pencil cup by the register. "Clip away."

When he was done, he pulled a small, silver hand bowl from his leather satchel and poured the holy water into it. Then he poured in the blessed salt, stirring the water with the rosemary sprigs as the salt flowed into the water and dissolved. Once the mixture was complete, Father Tony immersed the rosemary into the water, then walked to each window and door and flung the droplets against them. Then, he blessed both her apartment upstairs and the store on the ground level, by sprinkling the holy water in a path from the furthest window in the back, down the stairs and out the front door, driving any evil spirits in his path out of the building.

"I learned the last time I was here that the rosemary makes a better tool for dispersing holy water than my silver aspergillum," he said, setting down the sprigs and pulling the traditional holy water sprinkler from his bag to show her.

"And it provides additional protection," Jo said.

He gave her a puzzled glance.

"Rosemary protects against evil. I use it frequently in—" She'd been about to say *in my spells*, but she didn't want to start an argument with the priest. He knew what she practiced. There was no need to rub it in his face. She reached for the sprigs he'd used and started stripping the individual leaves from the stems. "You know, rosemary is sacred to Mary," she said.

"What?" Father Tony seemed more startled than interested, but she persisted.

"The flowers are blue. It's said that when Mary fled to Egypt, she spread her blue cloak on a rosemary bush to dry, and rosemary flowers have been blue ever since."

"I'm not sure—"

Jo found a piece of tissue under the counter and wrapped the rosemary leaves inside. She handed them to Father Tony with a small shrug. "Or, you could just sprinkle these in your sweater drawer to keep the moths away."

Their hands touched, and he grasped them with his own. "Your hands are so warm," he said. He leaned forward to touch her brow. "You're not just tired, you're burning up. We should get you to a doctor."

Yeah, well...she'd been down that path already.

"I saw the doctor a day ago and he did some tests." She slipped her hands out of his, and reached for her tea. "It's nothing more than a bug—a persistent bug." *A nasty, evil bug, brought on by demons.*

"Your eyes are getting glassy," Father Tony said. "I thought you looked tired when I walked in, but you're even worse-looking now."

"Thanks."

"I'm serious. You look like death warmed over."

She giggled. He had no idea how accurate he was.

"This isn't funny." The look he gave her was all stern schoolmaster and not at all helpful priest.

"I know that well," she said, sipping her tea.

He pulled the mug away from her once she'd sat it down on the counter. "And you shouldn't be drinking hot tea; you should be drinking iced water, or at least *iced* tea, you need something to bring the fever down."

He went to the small bathroom next to the counter and ran cold tap water in the sink, dumping the tea from her mug and filling it with the cool water, but letting the water continue to run. "Where do you keep your aspirin?"

"Basket on the back of the toilet."

She heard him rummage through the basket. He returned with the aspirin and the mug of cool water. "Take these." He laid the white tablets on the counter with the mug. Then, he grabbed the hand towel from the hook by the sink and soaked it in the running water. He wrung it out, folded it in half, brought it to Jo and placed it against her forehead. "Hold this against your brow."

She did as he bade, feeling immediate relief when the cool water touched her skin. She wasn't hopeful it would last.

"I still think we should get you back to the doctor," he said. "I don't like how hot you are."

"The doctor will just tell me to rest until he gets the test results."

Father Tony glared at her.

"Gosh you're stubborn. I'll take the aspirin and crawl into bed once you leave," Jo said. "Just turn the sign on the door to *Closed* on your way out."

"I don't like leaving you like this."

"I'm okay—really. I don't feel all that bad, just tired." *And hot. And sweaty from the fever. Plus, I'm dying. Very impractical—and it makes you think weird things.*

Slowly, he started packing up his priestly gear. "All right, but if I don't hear from you by dinner tonight, I'm coming back. And I'll drag you to the doctor again myself."

"I'm not one of your sheep."

"Assumpta is—so you are by association. Call me."

"Baa," she said, but she took the aspirin and promised to call.

CHAPTER 10

AFTER FATHER TONY LEFT, JO MADE CERTAIN the front door was locked before heading upstairs to her apartment. He was right—and she felt like crap. Maybe taking a day off would give her a chance to recoup some energy. Her customers could deal with a closed shop for a day or two.

It wasn't even noon yet, and she felt like she'd put in an entire day at the shop—unpacking inventory and on her feet for the duration. Those days were brutal, exhausting, and that's just how she felt now. Exhausted.

Dying has a way of doing that to you.

All she wanted to do was crawl into bed and sleep. But, first, a shower. She couldn't get into bed with fevery sweat all over her skin. She wanted to feel refreshed, and clean, and put on some fresh jammies— all of which she hoped would relax her enough to sleep. Since Father Tony had warded all the entrances, she was fairly confident nothing could harm her. She still wanted to do her own warding, but she felt safer than she had in days. Clean and secure—it was enough to lull anyone into a sound sleep—she hoped.

Jo started the water in the shower and let it run while she laid out fresh clothing and got undressed. She debated removing the scarab so it wouldn't get wet, but decided not to. Pournelle had warned her to keep it on. So, she let it dangle between her breasts, enjoying the heat of the copper as it warmed against her skin.

Steam curled out of the shower as she grabbed a fresh face cloth and towel from the minuscule bathroom cupboard. She draped the new towel over the curtain rod near the back of the tub where it would be out of the line of spray.

Suddenly drained, Jo needed all of her effort to lift her foot over the edge of the tub and step in. She leaned against the shower wall, letting the warm water spill over her, while she closed her eyes and breathed deeply of the steam. After a moment, she gathered her strength and pulled the curtain closed.

Dammit. Was she ever going to feel better? And what if she didn't? What if the scarab allowed her to keep on living, but she kept feeling more and more miserable? Who wants that kind of life? She had to do something to break this curse.

But she didn't have the energy, and she knew it. She couldn't do any research feeling like this. She could only hope that the longer she wore the scarab, the better she would feel. Soon maybe, she would feel like her old self—only with the understanding that she was dying.

The bed beckoned, but she still felt grimy and didn't want to carry that into the sheets with her. But there was no way she was going to manage a thorough cleansing—as much as she'd like to. At this point, she's settle for rinsing off the sweat, wrapping herself up in a comforter, and collapsing into bed. Still leaning against the wall for support, she grabbed the soap and lathered a cloth. Maybe she'd feel a little better if she washed her face. She lifted the cloth and scrubbed.

The water got too hot, and she reached blindly for the faucet. When she couldn't reach it, she leaned away from the wall, cursing her old Baltimore furnace for its temperamental proclivities. Dizziness assailed her. The washcloth fell from her hands.

The water got hotter, still—unnaturally hot—burning her, and Jo knew she couldn't blame the furnace anymore. Heart thumping, she reached for the faucet again, and slipped.

She cried out, grabbing for the curtain, and knocked her head against the wall.

Everything went black.

CHAPTER 11

ASSUMPTA HUNG UP THE PHONE FOR THE FOURTH time. She couldn't reach Jo.

Father Tony had called and relayed his conversation with Jo from earlier in the day. Jo hadn't called him, he'd said, and no one was picking up the phone at the shop. He was worried about her. And now, she was worried, too.

It would take her at least an hour to hop the next bus in rush hour traffic and get to Jo's. But she knew a faster way.

She went to her altar, flipped open her largest Bible, and reached for one of Pournelle's calling cards. She read his name aloud, "Pournelle Ahb —" As she said the words, the letters burned off the card, eventually catching the thick, white paper on fire. She rushed to the kitchen and dropped the burning paper into the stainless-steel sink.

"You again? I've got to find a way to block your summons," Pournelle said as he appeared in her kitchen.

"Because calling cards are so passé?"

"Because using them pulls me away from what I'm currently doing, and as you know, it's often inconvenient."

"So, get a cell phone." Assumpta looked at Pournelle, searching for a bloody dagger. It wouldn't be the first time that his *something inconvenient* involved a knife.

Pournelle smiled. "It's not what you're thinking. Get your mind out of Hell. You know, I do have other interests."

"Do tell." It might be fun to explore what Pournelle's *other interests* might be.

"I'm certain now isn't the time." He brushed some imaginary dust off his lapel. "Why did you call for me?"

"Father Tony called. He can't reach Jo—and neither can I."

"Father Tony and Jo?"

"I'll explain later," Assumpta said. "I've called her four times in the last hour and she's not returning my calls—not in the shop and not on her personal cell phone."

Pournelle immediately became concerned. "Why didn't you call me sooner?"

Because I'm getting a little too reliant on a demon to help me out?

"I didn't think I would need your help. I knew she was feeling bad when we'd seen her last. So, I thought she might be resting. But Jo's usually really good at returning my calls. I think we need to check on her—and you can get us there faster."

"Say no more." He snapped his fingers, and was gone.

Well, damn, she thought. She'd meant for Pournelle to take her with him. As much as she hated traveling by the snap of his fingers, she'd do it in a heartbeat for Jo.

Before she could blink, Pournelle was back, looking more worried than ever.

"What's wrong?"

"I couldn't get in. Jo has the place fully warded. Father Tony?"

Assumpta could've kicked herself. Of course Jo had the place warded. She had her own place warded—and she still checked every window, door and crack in the apartment each night to make sure that everything was still in place and the demons couldn't get in. "Yes— that's a good thing, right?"

He nodded. "If it can keep me out, it should keep practically everything else out, too."

"Did you knock?"

Pournelle gave her an affronted look. "Do you take me for a fool? Jo didn't answer the door when I knocked. And unless you want me to take you back there to beat the door down, I'm out of options."

At this point, beating down the door was what she felt like doing. But it wouldn't get them very far — especially if Jo was hurt—or something worse. She could call the police or an ambulance and let them break down the door. But they might not come without some certainty that Jo was actually there in the apartment. She didn't know if anything was even wrong. Things just *felt* wrong.

Maybe Jo had turned off the ringer on her phone. Maybe she was in such a deep sleep, she didn't hear Pournelle knocking on the door. But it would be out of character for Jo to do so.

Maybe, there was something else she could do. "Thank you. I guess I'll take it from here."

"That's it? You have no further need of my services? Perhaps I want to stick around and see for myself that Jo is all right." Pournelle straightened, making himself even taller. "Why do I suddenly feel used?"

Assumpta couldn't help but laugh. "Because that's what just happened?" *That's what true friends do: allow themselves to be used, because one day, they know they'll be the one doing the using.*

Jo had told her all about her and Pournelle's conversation about *friendship.* For as much as Pournelle wanted to be friends, he knew very little about friendship and how it worked. She took another look at him.

He looked angry. And maybe when she knew what was up with Jo, she could have this discussion with Pournelle. She raised her hand, halting his indignant speech. "Look, I don't have time for explanations, but I assure you that using each other is something that friends do all the time. The thing is, we usually see it the other way around: A friend will do anything for another friend. It's not really *using.* It's about being willing to ask and willing to give."

She approached her altar and struck a match, then set aflame the tall candle on the left, then the tall candle on the right, and said, "You can hang around if you want. I don't want you to feel like I'm dismissing you. But I'm going to call Saint Michael, and I didn't think you'd want to be around when I did."

"Do you think he'll come?"

She faced Pournelle, shaking out the match as she did so. "Why do you ask?"

She'd never told Pournelle that she and Saint Michael were on the outs. It would mean admitting to Pournelle that she had in her possession the medallion that controlled all demons. He'd wonder if she'd ever used it against him. She never had—had never even entertained the idea. But would he believe her? For whatever reason, she didn't want Pournelle to think poorly of her—didn't want to lose his *good will*—so she kept mum.

Saint Michael had abandoned her because she'd refused to give the medallion to him when he'd demanded it. She'd known the thing was demonic—and quite evil—but still hadn't been able to part with it at the time. And now she was stuck with it, and that quite likely amounted to an *eternal* sin on her soul—the worst sin possible, because eternal sins were unforgivable.

She sighed. After all that she'd been through, after finally getting rid of the demon mark, she was still probably headed straight for Hell.

Pournelle cleared his throat, bringing Assumpta out of her reverie. "You haven't mentioned him. And I haven't seen him around in a while. I figured you must have insulted him or something."

She nodded. "Yeah—something like that."

"You're right about me not wanting to be here when you call him. So, I'll take my leave now, and let you do your thing. I hope we're worried for nothing." Pournelle lifted his hand. "Please let me know if there's anything wrong with Jo—if there's anything I can do." And with a snap of his fingers, he was gone.

Assumpta grabbed a pillow from the couch to kneel on, knelt in front of her altar and crossed herself. It had been a while since she'd done this—where should she start?

Saint Michael had once told Assumpta that Mary always intervenes when asked, so maybe Mary was the best place to start. Because, now that she was alone, she was too chickenshit to call on Saint Michael himself.

She cleared her throat. "Dear Mary, I would like to beg an intercession from you. Pournelle and I—" *Should I even mention Pournelle here?* She started over. "*I* am very worried about my friend Jo. She has not been well, and I'm unable to reach her. I'm afraid that she's either very sick and can't let anyone know that she needs help or that she is in some kind of danger. Can you please ask Saint Michael to check—" Assumpta faltered. She wasn't clear on Mary's role here. She knew she could ask Mary to intercede with God for her, but could she ask Mary to talk with Saint Michael on her behalf? Now that she thought about it, probably not. She amended her prayer. "Dear Mary, can you please ask God to check, or send someone else to check, on Jo? I'm going to catch the crosstown bus and knock on Jo's apartment door myself. But in case I'm not going to get there in time, I beg that you ask for help for Jo. Thank you for your intercession. Amen."

Assumpta stood, dusted her knees and returned the throw pillow to the couch. She grabbed her purse and left.

CHAPTER 12

SAINT MICHAEL MATERIALIZED INSIDE JO'S apartment in his pagan guise of the Roman god Mars. He looked around briefly, heard the water running in the shower, and walked in that direction. He knocked on the bathroom door. "Jo?"

When she didn't answer, Mars knocked again, louder.

When she didn't answer the second time, he stepped *through* the door, much like a ghost. Gods didn't bother to turn doorknobs.

The small room was filled with steam and felt as hot as Hell. Jo lay in the bathtub, the downed shower curtain covering most of her torso and head. Scalding hot water rained down on her legs. The face cloth that Jo had dropped earlier lay half covering the drain. Hot water pooled in the tub up to her knees. Blisters were starting to form on her feet and ankles.

With a glance at the showerhead, Mars stopped the scalding water, and moved the facecloth out of the way. The water started to drain.

He walked back to the living room, found the phone, and dialed 9-1-1.

"9-1-1. Please state the nature of your emergency." The operator's tone was nasal and impatient.

"A woman has slipped in the bathtub and is unconscious. She is burned by the hot water. Be certain to come up the fire escape in the rear." There was no sense for the EMTs to run through her shop like bulls.

"What—?"

Mars ignored the other questions asked by the operator and rattled off Jo's street address, then he disconnected the phone, raised the window at the back by the fire escape and returned to the bathroom to wait with her.

Gently, he disentangled the shower curtain from Jo and draped it over the edge of the tub. Now that he could see her better, he noticed a small bruise forming on her temple. He reached out and touched her face, smoothing the pad of his thumb across the bruise, feeling the bump that was starting to rise. He said a few words under his breath, and the bruise disappeared along with the bump.

He placed his hand on Jo's forehead, felt the heat rising from her skin, and again said a few healing words. Her brow cooled immediately. Then it warmed again. Mars frowned, resting his hand for a longer time on her forehead. He said the healing words again, felt the brow cool and then warm. He probed deeper.

Sorrow filled him. He could cure the worst of the physical injuries, the bruise on her head—the concussion—most of the blistering. But the pervasive illness, *the evil*, he could do nothing for. Mars moved his hand to the top of her head and roused Jo in a dream state.

JO WOKE TO CLOUDS AND GRAY DARKNESS. FOG. Mist. It wasn't raining, but the air felt damp, almost wet, and cool. Her head was still pounding with fever, and she didn't know where she was. She stood, each movement more and more lethargic as she fought the sluggishness that had been plaguing her for days. The last thing she remembered was taking a shower. Could she be so exhausted that she didn't remember finishing and crawling into bed? She had to be dreaming.

So, she walked, because what else could she do?

As she walked, the fog and mist cleared, the sun came up and the air warmed, and Jo came to a large elm tree standing at the edge of an endlessly wide wheat field. The tall stalks, heavy with seed at the top, swayed slightly in a breeze she couldn't feel. The susurrus of the rubbing heads of wheat echoed across the otherwise silent field.

The pain in her head eased. She stood beneath the elm's branches, feeling cooler and less tired than during her walk, and stared at the Roman temple in the distance beyond the wheat.

Roman temple?

A figure walked toward her through the field, the waist-high wheat stalks parting before him. The symbolism was not lost on Jo. "Father Mars," she said, when he finally reached her. She bowed her head, afraid if she tried to bend at the waist she would fall.

He was tall and made even taller by the large, plumed helmet he wore. A red cloak was pushed back over his shoulders, exposing heavily muscled arms and the uniform of a Roman legionnaire. A sword hung at his waist.

He removed the helmet, revealing a man with light brown, curly hair and a curling beard. "I knew you would see the way of it," he said, smiling.

Jo nodded again, knowing she should show more deference to one of the old gods. The tableau made sense to her now. "To what do I owe the honor of this visit?"

"I am here because someone called to let me know you were in trouble."

Trouble? She tried to think. A wave of dizziness assailed her, and she put a hand out to steady herself against the tree. Rough bark scratched the palm of her hand. Moisture dotted her forehead. *Everything* felt all too real to be a dream, Jo thought, and yet, it could be nothing else.

A breeze blew and the wheat heads rubbing together sounded like song. Jo shivered, suddenly cold. She could feel her short, spiky hair slicked back with moisture. Cold water dripped down her neck. She was unclothed. *Skyclad.*

She looked down. Kernels of ripened wheat sifted beneath her bare feet, almost like sand. The wind blew across her damp body, and she was cool—cooler than she'd felt in a long time. It felt wonderful. She remembered the shower, the water getting hotter and hotter— scalding. She had felt—

Miserable. She had felt dizzy, even more so than she did now. She hadn't been able to hold herself upright. She hadn't been able to keep her balance, her head swimming—and hurting. She had reached for the shower curtain and had slipped, falling into the tub, banging her head against the tile.

She raised an open palm to her forehead, feeling where her head had struck the wall. She detected no wound, felt no pain.

"That injury was easy to take care of." Mars turned away, looking across the wheat fields, as if he didn't want to speak but knew he must. "It's the other—the illness—that I can't help you with."

"Is it so obvious to everyone that I am not feeling well?"

Mars turned back to her and shook his head. "No, it's not that you're not feeling well; it's that you are *very* sick." She could tell that he didn't want to tell her, but he did. "You're dying."

Jo nodded. She knew that already. Was this repetition her mind simply accepting that fact, or was she really talking with Mars? What was so important that he graced her with his presence?

He continued, "The problem, Jo, is that there is nothing I can do to help. The illness you suffer from is *unnatural.* My powers aren't enough to heal that."

Mars reached for a stalk of wheat and broke it off. He stripped the heavy seeds by running his fingers up the shaft. They dropped to the ground, and almost immediately sprouts grew up around his feet.

"They're almost here, so I need to be going." He gave her a sad look. "They'll treat your symptoms, but they, too, will fail to make a cure."

"Who's almost here?"

"The paramedics. I had to leave some burns on your legs from sitting in the scalding water, or they would get suspicious. Assumpta is on her way to your apartment. When you see her at the hospital, reassure her that she has done everything she could for you—she has. She will believe that that she did not call soon enough." He paused, as if debating whether to say more. Then, he said, "Also, tell her when you see her that the sin she carries is not *in extremis* so long as she repents and takes care of the problem. The scope—"

"Sin *in extremis?*"

"She'll know what I mean. I have to go. Regarding your unnatural illness, find the source, only then can you be made well."

"But—"

"Find the source. Destroy it." He began fading from her vision. "I have to be going."

Clouds rolled across the sky. The daylight faded, and fog rolled in, enveloping Mars and obliterating him from Jo's view. The great dark wind blew in more darkness until it was all around her.

The darkness became complete, and Jo felt nothing.

FROM THE BATHROOM, MARS HEARD THE pounding of booted feet running up the metal fire escape.

"Paramedics!" yelled a baritone voice through the window.

There was a thump, as something heavy hit the floor in the hallway, and then three sets of booted feet raced to the bathroom.

Mars, back in his guise of Saint Michael, melted away as the paramedics entered.

CHAPTER 13

FOUR HOURS LATER, ASSUMPTA SAT ON A LOVE seat in Jo's living room and kicked off her shoes. She was exhausted from having followed the ambulance to the hospital and waiting for Jo to be treated. Jo had regained consciousness in the ambulance as they'd sped their way along the city streets, and the examination had showed nothing seriously wrong—except for the burns—so the hospital had released her once they'd treated them.

With Jo in no shape to make it home on her own, Assumpta had taken control. She'd called a cab, helped Jo to her bedroom when they arrived, and given her one of the prescribed pain pills before settling down on the short couch to get some sleep.

It seemed that no sooner had she closed her eyes than Pournelle appeared beside the love seat opposite Assumpta's. "Wakey-wakey."

Assumpta sat up, proud of herself—she'd hardly been startled at all. She was almost getting used to Pournelle's sudden comings and goings. "Eggs and bac-y?"

As if on cue, Assumpta's stomach rumbled. She couldn't have timed that better.

Pournelle rolled his eyes, but he snapped his fingers. A golden-brown croissant appeared on a plate in her lap. The smell of butter assailed her, and Assumpta's mouth watered. She picked it up. "It's still warm!"

"Let's not make a habit of this."

Assumpta took a bite of the croissant, and the promised buttery goodness filled her mouth. She took another. "Wait—" she swallowed and said, "I thought you couldn't *snap* yourself into this apartment—the place was too warded."

Pournelle smiled. "There was enough traffic back-and-forth over the window threshold that it erased all the warding Jo put there. I waltzed in here just as easily as you did. Easier, actually."

Assumpta frowned, wishing she'd thought of that. She should have re-warded the window after she'd settled Jo. She was all-too-familiar with warding that had failed to do its job. Early on in her association with demons, the warding on her own apartment door had failed to keep the demons out. If it had not been for Jak, she would've been dead.

Jak. She no longer pined for what couldn't be, but she couldn't help the small bit of melancholy his name still evoked. She pushed it aside. "I'm surprised you want to hang out here, with all the other wards in place."

"So long as no one tries to seal me in here permanently, there'll be no problems. But I have a hunch, and we need to search this joint."

"Search for what?"

"For whatever it is that's making Jo ill." Pournelle bent to the loveseat closest to him and started lifting cushions. He tucked his hands into folds and corners, obviously looking for something. When he found nothing, he moved to the love seat Assumpta occupied. "Move."

Assumpta glared at him but moved to the hearth. "I thought you said she was—" *Dying.* She didn't want to say the word aloud, as if not voicing it could keep it from happening. She cleared her throat, started again. "I though you said Jo was dying from a demon curse."

"She is," Pournelle said, "but there's got to be something else, as well. Something making her sick on top of the curse. The scarab is protecting her against the death spell, but it's not designed to work against more than that. Ergo—" He forced the cushion down and moved to the next. "—there must be something else."

"Unbelievable." Assumpta rubbed her eyes, then dropped her hands to her lap. She picked at the croissant. "So you're saying that even though the scarab is keeping her alive, she'll continue to be miserably ill anyway?"

"Precisely—until we find the charm that's making her sick and destroy it."

"How do you know there's a charm? Maybe your scarab just doesn't work as well as you think it should."

"The scarab is working just fine."

"But how do you know?"

He glared at her. "I just do."

"You can't just *know* something." Assumpta gave him an assessing look. "What aren't you telling me?"

Pournelle blew out a deep breath and looked at his shoes. Softly, he said, "There aren't any wards in public places. I didn't want her to be unprotected in the hospital. They wouldn't let you stay with her while they treated her, but they couldn't object to what they couldn't see. Namely me."

Assumpta found herself smiling. "You sat with her."

"I watched *over* her."

"That still doesn't tell me how you know the scarab is working and how her illness is related to something else."

"All it takes is a touch." He opened the small drawer of the occasional table by the love seat and rummaged through its contents. "I knew it then."

"A small touch?"

He slammed the drawer shut. "As when my hand brushed hers the first time and I discovered the demonic necrosis."

Assumpta thought about that. Pournelle was probably telling her the truth about touching Jo and discovering this new thing. But why not just come out and say it? He was still hiding something. And then it dawned on her. The touch. "You held Jo's hand!"

He froze, then answered stiffly. "I may have offered her some comfort while she was alone—as any friend might do."

"There's no need to be embarrassed."

"Demons *do not* get embarrassed. And I'm done with this conversation."

Still smiling, Assumpta said, "Fine. But how do you know it's a charm and not another spell."

"Logic."

She gave him a puzzled look.

"It can only be a charm because demon spells come at a cost. They require effort, and demons are basically lazy. Why go through the motions—pay the price—of performing another spell when a charm can be almost as effective?"

Assumpta's head was beginning to pound, and it wasn't just from fatigue. She closed her eyes and rubbed her temples, trying to alleviate the headache. "Then why didn't the demons just create a death charm?"

Pournelle stood up straight. "Because there's no such thing as a death charm." He said it matter-of-factly—as if any idiot would know that. But he must have seen the look of frustration on her face, because he clarified, "It isn't possible to imbue an object with enough power to kill. That takes *serious* magic. Charms are easy. They're one of the first magics a demon learns."

"They've effectively already killed Jo—since we don't know of a way to break the spell. All they have to do is wait Jo out. Steal the scarab. Why would they go to the effort at all?"

"Because they can. Besides, it's an easy way to cause more harm. Don't think they aren't enjoying this. It's all a game to them."

Assumpta suddenly felt powerless. She took another bite of the croissant, buying some time so she could decide what to do. Maybe she should just confront the demons and try to clear up this mess. It had worked for her in the past.

"You could help, you know."

"I don't know," Assumpta said. "I don't feel right looking through Jo's things. It's an invasion of privacy. I know I wouldn't like it if you went through my stuff."

"Going through *your* things could get me killed." Pournelle straightened up the cushions on the sofa and moved to the bric-a-brac on the mantle above the fireplace. He searched for concealed items behind framed pictures, opened canisters and looked into vases. "But I'd still do it if it meant saving your life. And I'm sure you'd be happy about it, as I think Jo will be, too."

Assumpta ignored the bit about Pournelle admitting he'd risk his own life for hers. She'd give it more thought later, when she had time. "You didn't say you were going to save her life—you said you had a hunch. But, okay, I'm willing, what is it I'm looking for?"

"I'm not certain." Pournelle moved to the bookshelf and gave it the same kind of once over, opening each book one-by-one and fanning the pages as well. "But if my hunch is correct, we should be looking for something *witchy*. Demons like to hide things in plain sight."

Assumpta chuckled. "Could you be a little more specific? Since Jo's a witch, I'm certain we'll find quite a few *witchy* things around here."

"Jo's a good witch—her possessions will lean towards neutral or good. We're looking for something that leans toward evil, in fact, it will be most definitely, demonically evil—but it will likely *look* witchy, so it doesn't stand out too much among Jo's things."

"I still don't know what I'm looking for."

"I contend you'll know it when you see it," Pournelle said. "And I'm not seeing anything." He slammed a cabinet door. "I'll bet it's in her bedroom." He crossed his arms on his chest, and gave Assumpta a pointed stare. "You'll need to go in there and look."

"You draw the line of privacy invasion at the bedroom door?"

"Actually, no—but I think Jo might, even in this instance."

"She's resting—hopefully asleep. I don't want to disturb her."

"Disturb her now or go to her funeral later. Your choice."

"You said the charm was only making her sick!"

"Sicker and sicker!" Pournelle shouted. "Draw your own conclusions."

"We could do it my way, so we don't disturb Jo anymore," Assumpta said, setting aside the plate and retrieving her pendulum from her purse. She was a *finder* after all. She tugged on the string, straightening it, then let the clear teardrop-shaped crystal bead dangle on the end of its tether. "Is there something here in Jo's apartment which is making her ill?"

The pendulum hung slack while Assumpta and Pournelle watched. It did nothing.

Pournelle regarded Assumpta with an impatient stare, folding his arms on his chest while he waited.

After a moment of the pendulum's inaction, Assumpta tried again. "Will you help us find the bespelled item which is making Jo ill?"

Again, there was no movement from the pendulum.

"I don't understand," Assumpta said.

Pournelle shrugged. "I was afraid it wasn't going to work."

"Why didn't you say something?

"I didn't want you to think I had something to do with it." He moved to the bookcase and started looking again. "Maybe Jo's got the place so warded—minus the doorway, now—that nothing can get in to help you. Or, maybe the charm is blocking any chance of aid."

"Maybe the spirits just aren't feeling cooperative," Assumpta said. Her shoulders slumped. She shoved the pendulum into her pocket.

Pournelle's back was to her when her spoke. "I'll keep looking out here, while you search her room."

Assumpta nodded. "Right."

She walked down the short hallway to Jo's room and pushed open the door. Jo lay on the bed propped up on a few pillows. She wore light pajamas and had a small lap robe covering her hips, but her legs were bare. In the dim light, Assumpta could see that the doctor had spread thick white cream on them from the tops of her knees down to her feet.

It was her fault. Because she was friends with Jo, Jo got hurt. She had to make things right. And going forward, she had to stop the demons—stop anyone else from getting hurt. But first, she had to find whatever it was that was making Jo ill.

So where should she look? It couldn't be hidden somewhere obvious, because otherwise Jo would've found it already.

There was enough light coming in from the shaded window to see around the room, but not enough if she wanted to dig under the bed and look through the closet. And she didn't want to disturb Jo by turning on the light. She stepped out of the room.

"Now what?" Pournelle asked her. He had the look of a disapproving father on his face, like she disobeyed him for the very last time—like she couldn't get anything right—and this was the last straw.

"I need a flashlight."

Pournelle grumbled almost inaudibly, but snapped his fingers and one appeared in his hand. He offered it to Assumpta. She took the flashlight and went back into the bedroom, aiming the light downward and flicking it on. She started in the closet, opening the door as softly as she could and stooping to look through the shoes first. She sighed. Unlike her, Jo had about a zillion pairs to dig through: flirty sandals; little boat shoes in blue-and-tan and white; black boots ranging from ankle height to thigh high and about a thousand pairs of flip-flops with daisies and beads and bows and more. Assumpta up-ended the boots and tennis shoes, looked behind a tripod and some camera equipment, and opened a decoupaged box containing what looked like a bunch of journals or diaries. Assumpta put the lid back on without touching those.

If she and Pournelle couldn't find anything else in the apartment, she'd have him do the dirty-work of riffling through these books. No way was she going through any of Jo's personal diaries—especially ones she had hidden away.

Assumpta found nothing in the shoes.

Several pocketless caftans in soft, flowing cottons and jersey hung on the right side of the closet. Beside them were long, flowy skirts in black and mocha and a few other dark colors. Colorful tops hung in the center of the closet, all made out of the same comfortable materials as the skirts. Two pair of jeans hung on the left, and pushed way to the back like a dirty, little secret, Assumpta found a suit jacket and matching skirt in black. It looked like it had never been worn.

Smiling at the suit, Assumpta checked every pocket she could find and even felt through the clothing, squeezing and brushing, to make certain nothing had been hidden up a shirt sleeve or tied to a belt. Nothing there either.

She closed the closet door again, as quietly as possible, and got down on her hands and knees, aiming the flashlight beam behind the night stand, and then sweeping it under the bed. There was nothing under the bed. Nothing. Not even any dust bunnies. She was jealous for a few seconds, then reminded herself that Jo had recently moved in. There hadn't been time for any dust bunnies to grow.

She panned the beam once more under the bed just in case she'd missed something tiny or something flat—something *unobtrusive*, as Pournelle might say.

Nothing beneath the bed, but the beam flashed against something on the far wall of the room, something below the radiator squatting under the window in the center of the wall. Something shiny.

Assumpta walked to the radiator and stepped on a squeaky board.

CHAPTER 14

"WHO'S THERE?" JO ASKED FROM THE BED, HER voice tired and thin. Wispy, as if only a part of Jo laid in the bed. She sounded so frail—and exhausted.

Assumpta frowned, but continued walking to the far wall and knelt beside the radiator. As if she hadn't felt bad enough already, she'd had to go and wake Jo when Jo seriously needed some restful sleep. *Great.*

"It's just me," Assumpta said. "Sorry to wake you." The bed squeaked and she heard some cover rustling. Assumpta realized Jo was getting up. "Jo—please, go back to sleep. I think I've found what Pournelle and I have been looking for."

There was a sigh—as if in relief—and then a small cough. The sheets rustled again as Jo laid back down. "Fill me in later."

And just like that, Assumpta felt ten times worse. Jo was so exhausted—so worn out—that she wasn't even questioning Assumpta's foray into her private space. Wait until Jo found out she'd pawed through her closet.

A moment later, soft snores came from the bed.

Assumpta pointed the flashlight beam under the radiator where the pipe led down into the floor. The beam revealed something shiny. Something small, in the open, yet concealed. This had to be it. Who would look under the radiator? She'd had to get down on her hands and knees and shine a flashlight to even see it. Then again, maybe Jo had just dropped something, and it had rolled under the radiator.

Assumpta reached for the object and nearly touched it, her fingers almost grazing the shiny thing—then, she reconsidered. If it was the charm, was it safe to touch? If close proximity was enough to make Jo ill, what would it do to her if she touched it? She pulled her sleeve down to cover her hand and reached for it.

It was larger than she'd thought. The shiny bit was only a part of the whole, Assumpta realized, as her fingertips bumped against something round and obviously dark, camouflaged in the shadows. She opened her hand wider and grabbed hold.

"Got it," she said quietly, giving it a tug. It was stuck, held fast to the radiator by something. *Yes*, it had to be the charm. She yanked harder, heard a snapping sound as whatever held it fastened broke apart, and then she held it in her hand. The entire charm was slightly larger than a golf-ball, smooth and hard—and wet. Had she broken the radiator? Assumpta aimed the flashlight on the floor beneath the radiator and then on the radiator itself. No water. Nothing seemed amiss. So where was the damp feeling coming from?

She pulled the charm closer to her and shined the flashlight on it.

A twist of broken vine curled around a horse chestnut. One of Jo's earrings—at least, she assumed it was one of Jo's earrings—had been tied to the nut with the vine. It hardly looked evil. Until she turned it over. The nut was hollowed out and pressed inside was the severed head of a small rodent. Blood dripped down on her hand.

Assumpta screeched.

"What?" Jo sat up in bed. "What's going on?"

"Nothing," Assumpta said, fighting the urge to wipe her hand on the area rug. She got to her feet and made her way to the door. "Go back to sleep. I've got it."

Jo relaxed again, and Assumpta left the room and walked down the short hallway. "I've got it," she repeated, louder, making her way into the living room. She held the broken vine between two fingers, letting the chestnut dangle down a few inches from her bloodied hand.

Pournelle reached for it, also grasping it by the wispy vine. "Let me see it."

"Mind the rat's head," Assumpta said, handing it over. "I don't think it's fastened particularly well." She resisted the impulse to wipe her hand on her pants and grabbed a tissue from a nearby box. She wiped her palm and grimaced at the drying rat blood which wouldn't come off her sleeve. "Have you ever seen anything like this before?"

"Not exactly like this." Pournelle laid the chestnut on Jo's coffee table, rat head up. "I presume the earring is Jo's. It's normal to have something from the cursed to bind the charm with." Pournelle untied the string that had bound the charm to the radiator and the earring to the charm, then tugged the rat head from the center of the nut.

"What are you doing?"

"Dismantling it."

"And that will take care of the spell?"

"It should." Once Pournelle had reduced the charm to the sum of its parts, he laid them in the fireplace. "But we'll burn them up just to be certain."

"Jo's earring, too?"

"We could wait for Jo's permission, but I'm certain she'll agree that it's the best course," Pournelle said.

"Burn away," Jo said softly from the hallway. Pournelle and Assumpta turned to face her.

"Let me help you to the sofa," Assumpta said, approaching her.

Jo raised her hand and waved away her help. "I can do it." She trudged wearily to the loveseat and sat down. "Burn everything," she said. "And while you're at it, make another sweep of the house, if you don't mind.

"We can do that," Pournelle said, "but it's probably pointless. It only takes one."

"Okay—if you're certain." Jo nodded. "Matches are in the vase on the mantle."

"Not necessary," Pournelle said. He raised his hand and snapped. Immediately, all four pieces of the charm burst into flames, even Jo's metal earring. The smell of burnt fur and animal flesh, as well as iron and the woodsy aroma of the nut and vine, filled the room.

Jo covered her mouth and nose and looked away.

Assumpta coughed. "Oh, that's awful."

"But done." The flames died away, leaving four small piles of ashes. Pournelle pointed into the firebox, rotating his hand in a circle. As he did so, a small dust devil swirled around and around, gathering all the ashes together. Pournelle snapped his fingers, and the entire mess *whooshed* up the chimney.

"That's the cleanest my fireplace has ever been," Jo said. "But is it okay to co-mingle the ashes? It can't somehow form into some secondary ash charm, can it?"

"No need to worry." Pournelle sat on the loveseat across from Jo. "As soon as all the pieces burned the charm was consumed and the magic nullified. Mixing the ashes means nothing." He looked her up and down. "How do you feel?"

"Spent. Queasy—but not as *heavy* as I've been feeling lately. Shouldn't I feel better than this?"

"Not necessarily. The charm was making you sick. So, you're sick. It might take a few days before you feel better. Breaking the charm doesn't make you any less sick than you already are. So now, you'll just have to get well." He grinned at her, his familiar Chicklet smile bright against the darkness of his face.

"Except I'm dying."

"Not while you're wearing the scarab," Pournelle said.

"But I'm *still* dying."

Assumpta reached for one of Jo's hands and held it between her own. "Sure, you're dying," she said with a shrug. "We're *all* dying. You just happen to know that your time is up soon. But—" She said the last with a sharp, annunciation of the word, and then repeated it. "But—you've also got a scarab that's keeping things in check. And you've got some knowledge of what's going on and how to stop it. And now that you're not sick anymore, you'll soon have the energy to reverse this Hellish spell—"

"And so we should let you rest." Pournelle snapped his fingers and a pillow and blanket appeared on the loveseat next to Jo.

"But I'd like to talk to you about—"

"Rest," Pournelle insisted. He reached into his vest pocket and pulled out a white card. "Call on me when you get hungry. I'm certain I can conjure something up." He grinned again, then stood and held his hand out to Assumpta. She grasped it, he snapped, and then they were back at her apartment, standing outside the door.

Assumpta hadn't needed to clasp his hand, of course, but Pournelle was nothing, if not dramatic—especially about entrances and exits.

CHAPTER 15

JO WOKE.

Dim light filtered in through the Venetian blinds, bathing the room in early dawn.

After Pournelle and Assumpta had left in the wee hours of the morning, she'd laid on the sofa for a while, dozing off and on. She'd thought a lot about the broken charm and a little about her visit from the pagan god Mars. She'd wanted to discuss it with Pournelle and Assumpta, but they hadn't given her the opportunity.

She hadn't wanted to eat and had desired company even less, so she'd ignored Pournelle's directive to call on him and made her way back to the bedroom where she'd promptly fallen asleep. Until now.

And thoughts of Mars' visit crowded her mind again.

Had he actually come to her? Or had it just been a dream? She wasn't entirely certain.

She'd never been religious having been raised that religion was little more than myth. But even now realizing that a god exists—Assumpta's god—it didn't compel her to worship *Him*. She couldn't, not when His teaching and her pagan way of life were at odds with each other.

But Mars—he was an *old god*. Her belief and ritual slotted together nicely with his existence. Did that mean she should now begin worshiping Mars?

He'd confirmed what Pournelle had told her—that she was dying—which was the very thing that made her wonder if his appearance was simply her mind playing tricks on her. After all, she'd already known that. But Mars had also given her a message for Assumpta. That still could have been her mind playing tricks, but it had felt real enough to be true. And she didn't know about sins *in extremis*. She didn't know that such a thing even existed. Sin was sin, after all, right?

She sat up, feeling only slightly woozy, and reached for the scarab at her throat. Still there. She pushed back the covers on the bed and swung her feet to the floor, assessing. The mild dizziness was annoying, but she could work with it. It was certainly much less extreme than she'd experienced yesterday.

Her stomach growled, and she actually *felt* hungry. She'd take that as a good sign. She scanned the tops of her knees, her thighs. The burns on her legs weren't as bad as she thought they might be. The scarab at work? Or Mars? Maybe both. Either way, it was cause for celebration. She was on the mend—as much as she could be on the mend while still dying.

All in all, she felt and looked better than she thought she would this morning. She was capable of working *and* studying. It was time she figured out how to break a death spell, even if she had to go through every damned book in her library and then some.

Slipping her feet into hot pink bunny slippers, Jo stood and made her way to the small galley kitchen.

All was quiet, even the road traffic, which told her it was still early. That was good. She liked getting a head start on the day. She pulled a box of Oolong loose tea off the top shelf and measured out a full pot. She was going to need it. She set the kettle to boil and went to get dressed.

Half an hour later, she was downstairs in the shop feeling somewhat revived. Her spiky hair was still damp from a shower, another cup of tea was at her elbow, and the first stack of books was piled up in front of her—all of which had proved useless. She needed to discover more information about the demon death spell. Information about demons seemed easy to come by, but information about demon magic? Not so much. *Apparently, humans who dabbled in it didn't live long enough to write about it,* she thought. *If I live long enough, maybe I'll write a book to help out the next poor soul in this predicament.*

Jo worked through several more books, starting with the indexes, and moving on to the tables of contents if none existed. Books that might hold a clue, but no way to find it other than reading straight through, she set aside for later perusal. She wasn't reading for leisure here. She was on a mission to find out as much as she could, as fast as she could. Who knew how much longer she had to live, even with Pournelle's scarab as protection?

Speaking of Pournelle, he seemed to have a steady source of power to conjure things up: a business card or sandwich; tea for three, delicious and piping hot—all at the snap of a finger. He could transport himself, and someone else, clear across the city in the blink of an eye. Were these just parlor tricks? Perhaps they were simply minor magics that any demon could perform.

With luck, the really powerful spells that demons cast—anything more than those similar to Pournelle's *simple* tricks—required demons to draw their power from components and ritual like witches did. *Like the charm that had made her ill.* If so, it meant that demon spells were just as vulnerable to outside forces as her own. And whatever death spell the demons had cast on her could be unraveled like the charm—or nullified with some counter spell.

But Pournelle hadn't said as much. With a sinking feeling, she thought back to the last conversation with him and Assumpta. In fact, Pournelle had interrupted Assumpta when she'd suggested that Jo would soon feel better enough to look for a *cure.* Did he purposefully disrupt that chain of thought?

Was there no antidote to a demon death spell?

Jo slammed shut the book she'd been perusing. Why was she wasting her time here? She had the ultimate source practically at her fingertips. She pushed a button on the cash register and the drawer popped open with a *ding*. She lifted the money tray and pulled out one of Pournelle's calling cards.

CHAPTER 16

POURNELLE'S BUSINESS CARD WAS CRISP AND white and made of the heaviest paper Jo had ever felt. It was rich and smooth, and almost seemed wasteful to take advantage of it. She rubbed a thumb over the fine linen surface, almost caressing the raised gold leaf that spelled out Pournelle's full name.

"Pournelle Ahb—"

As Jo spoke his name aloud, the gold letters burst into flame and burned off the card—setting afire the fine linen-like material. Almost before she uttered the last syllable—the card a conflagration—Pournelle appeared on the other side of the front counter.

"Bloody Hell!"

Jo dropped the burning card to the glass-topped surface, where the flames extinguished themselves. The ash danced away from the fanning of her mildly scorched fingers.

Pournelle's hands were full with bloody intestines. He juggled the innards, one long loopy length of them sliding down to his wingtip shoes and dripping blood onto Jo's hardwood floor. "How is it that you and Assumpta always seem to call me at the most inopportune times?"

Jo swallowed. "Are you holding what I think you are holding?"

"Deer entrails." He said it with disgust, but Jo was certain it was with her and not the bloody guts. Pournelle shoved the whole sloppy mess under his left arm—another loop of intestines fell to the floor—and tried to snap his fingers. Blood slid between them dampening, the sound. Nothing happened.

"Bloody. *Hell.*" He stared at his right hand, glanced down at his pants—grimaced—and wiped his palm briskly on the navy, pinstriped material. He snapped his fingers again. This time, the snap rang out clear and loud.

Instantly, the entrails were gone—blood and gore with them—the pinstripe suit was pristine, the cuffs of his shirt blindingly white. Pournelle brushed some imaginary lint from his left shoulder and glared at Jo. "Now then, what do you want?"

Jo smiled at Pournelle. "Yes, I'm feeling much better today, thank you for asking. And thank you for your help."

He frowned. "I was in the middle of something when you called. I need to get back to it."

"You need to get back to bloody deer entrails? Surely they can wait."

"*They* can," Pournelle said, crossing his arms over his chest. "But the person waiting for them is in a hurry."

That brought her up short. "You deliver deer entrails on a regular basis?"

"Only when deer are in season."

Deer season? She blinked. "Let's start over. Tea?" Jo turned to the electric kettle behind her and turned it on.

"A moment," he said, snapping his fingers and disappearing.

He returned a few moments later, seeming less anxious. He waved a hand, clicking off Jo's teapot, and snapped his fingers. A small silver samovar, along with two delicate, gold-edged tea cups, appeared between the piles of books on her counter. A dish of sliced lemons and another of sugar cubes sat on the closest pile of books. A beautiful China tea pot, hand-painted with delicate, green rosemary sprigs yielding tiny blue flowers, sat on top of the samovar. Almost beneath her nose, the teapot emitted the fresh aroma of black, pekoe tea—one of her favorites.

"This is faster," he said, pulling a stool around and sitting. "Besides, you need your rest."

"I can make tea!"

"I know," he said, "but allow me." He nodded at her stool. "Get off your feet for a while. I'll bet you've been at this all morning." She glared at him but took a seat. He was right—she hadn't sat since she opened the store this morning. She leaned against the counter and reached for lemon as Pournelle filled their cups from the pretty rosemary-painted teapot.

He sipped. "So, what gives?"

"I've been going about my research all wrong," she said, twisting the lemon into her cup. "I've got a prime source right in front of me, and I haven't taken advantage of it."

"Prime source?"

"First-hand," Jo said, smiling. "Horse's mouth, as it were."

"Horse's mouth—*me?*"

"Exactly." She reached for her notebook and turned to a fresh page. "Tell me everything you know about the demon death spell. Anything which will help me break it. Do you mind if I write while we talk?"

"I've already told you all I know." Pournelle set the teacup gently on the counter and reached inside his jacket. He pulled out another calling card. "Of course, if I hear anything more, you'll be the first to know." He laid the card near the sugar cubes and stood. "Everyone in Hell has been so tight-lipped lately. Ferreting out anything is taking me some time. I could call in favors, but then they'll want to know why *I* want to know who's behind this."

"You misunderstand," Jo said. "After giving this some thought, I don't think it matters who has cast the spell—"

"Of course it matters."

Jo nodded. "Yes, of course it matters, but not in the short term. Right now, all I care about is breaking their spell. I don't know if that's even possible. I *hate* feeling this way. I don't need to know who cast the spell—yet. I just need to know how demon magic works," Jo said. "If I know how you guys do what you do, then maybe I can counter the spell in some way. Then I can heal. Once I feel better, we can take on the responsible parties."

There was silence between them for a long moment before Pournelle answered her. "I'm afraid I can't help you with that."

"*What?*" Shock froze her where she sat. *He'll help, but only so far? Why won't he take the next step?* Jo felt her mouth hanging open like a surprised fish. "Is there some kind of demon rule about not teaching outsiders about magic?"

"Something like that," Pournelle murmured quietly, staring down into his tea. He took a long drink, then set the cup on the counter. "Wait here—I have an idea."

He snapped his fingers and was gone again.

"As if I had a choice," Jo muttered to the suddenly empty room, setting her own cup down. She cleared the lemon and the sugar, sitting the small bowls on the low shelf next to her electric kettle, but left the samovar—with the pretty teapot on top—within easy reach. She freshened her cup, tucked Pournelle's new card back into the cash register, turned back a page in her notebook, and cracked open the next likely-looking tome.

While she waited for Pournelle, she helped three customers, drinking tea all the while, wondering which cup from the teapot was going to be the last. Somehow, it never seemed to empty. And the samovar seemed to contain an endless supply of hot water.

Jo filled an entire page in her notebook with speculative information about demon magic, some of it in direct contradiction with other bits. She threw down her pen and slammed the book shut, growling. She didn't know what to believe.

Just before noon, Pournelle walked through the front door, the odor of fried onions clinging to him. He set a greasy bag upon the counter and pulled out a large steak sub, the wrapper dripping in grease.

"Did you get some answers along with your sub?" Jo asked flipply.

"Better," Pournelle said. He snapped his fingers and a stack of fluffy paper towels appeared on the counter by the sub. "But first, we eat."

"Why are you always trying to take care of me?" Jo clutched her mug.

"Because you need a keeper?" Pournelle grinned and unrolled the paper enveloping the sub. He smoothed it down on the counter's surface, making a tablecloth of sorts, and then reached into the bag and pulled out a smaller, greasier brown bag. He tore the top off, and dumped a mound of steaming French fries next to the sub.

"I don't need a keeper."

"No more than the average human."

Jo glared at him, and he laughed.

"Look, after I left here, I spent a few hours in Hell trying to dig up information. I'd skipped breakfast and I was hungry. Don't eat if you don't want anything, but I thought it would be impolite to have lunch without bringing enough for two."

Jo glared harder, ignoring his reference to visiting Hell. He was a demon. It shouldn't really bother her, right? Yet it did, just a tiny bit. But she was more bothered by the fact that he thought she needed to be coddled. "You're really hungry? You didn't just bring enough food to feed an army, because you think I need to eat?"

He chuckled. "I'm that hungry." And when he realized she was glaring at him again, he added, *"Really."*

She nodded, accepting the explanation. "Let me close the store for lunch today since you're making such a mess." Pournelle frowned at her, but when she stood to fasten the door, he lifted his hand and snapped. The lock on the door *snicked* shut and the sign flipped over from *Open* to *Closed*.

Jo just shook her head and sat down, reaching for her tea.

"You won't eat?" Pournelle asked.

Jo shrugged and grabbed a fry. "I'm not hungry."

Pournelle took a huge bite of his sub, and that's when it dawned on her.

"Demons don't eat."

He chewed and swallowed, staring at the French fries. *Avoiding her gaze?*

"Who said?"

She looked over the counter and tapped a book. "This book." She tapped another. "And this one." She motioned to the shelf of books over the window. "I can pull down half a dozen more which say the same thing." She gave him a shrewd look. "Have you ever had lunch with Assumpta?"

Pournelle sat up straight, set the sub down and dusted his hands. "Maybe I've just never been hungry in her presence." He snapped his fingers, and everything related to lunch disappeared. The door unlocked, and the *Closed* sign flipped over to *Open*.

Oh, no, she'd pissed him off. *What happens now?*

Jo almost breathed a sigh of relief as Pournelle's next movement was fairly innocuous. He reached into his hip pocket, withdrew a burgundy-colored, leather-bound book slightly larger than an average paperback—though a bit thicker in width—and stood. Holding the book in the palms of his hands, he bent at the waist and offered it to Jo. "Demon to witch, I bestow this gift. May it always be where you think you've left it."

Jo stood, wiped her hands on a napkin and accepted the book with a bit of trepidation. Pournelle had just cast a spell—*may it always be where you think you've left it*. And he was formally *giving* her the book. She'd seen this kind of brief ceremony before—this was no loan. "What do you mean, '*may it always be where you think you've left it.*'?"

She ran an index finger over the foiled and gilt stamped letters on the cover. She couldn't read the words, couldn't even hazard a guess at the language it might be written in. A blood-red gemstone, about the size of a quarter was affixed to the front in a cradle of leather. It sat beneath the title like an unblinking eye.

"You don't want to lose a book like this," Pournelle said. "I merely ensured that it would always be in your possession—until you decide to give it back. Or give it away."

"Okaaaay," she said, drawing the word out and cracking open the book. *That sounded ominous.* But she couldn't help feeling a teensy bit excited about having a new book. A new *research* book. If she could translate the language, there was no telling what she might learn.

Smiling, she placed her thumb against the dark edge of the pages and fanned them—there had to be a thousand or more in the compact, little volume. She felt a sharp pain.

"Ouch!" A drop of blood formed on her thumb, and she felt oddly compelled to wipe it along the paper. Without thinking, she placed her thumb against the stacked edges again and dragged it upward from bottom to top, bracing herself for another *bite*. Instead, the blood was immediately absorbed, deepening the ochre-colored edges. Now she knew why the edges were rust-colored.

"Good," Pournelle said. "You felt the instinct to feed it. It's accepted you."

A prickle of fear washed down her spine and she shivered, suddenly chilled. She wasn't so excited any longer. "And that's a good thing?"

He nodded. "Now you can't possibly lose it."

"If you say so," she muttered, returning her attention to the book. "I'll have to keep feeding it?"

"No, just this once."

Thank Heaven for small favors, she thought, wishing he had warned her about the strange ritual of bonding with the book.

She opened the cover, and took a more careful look inside. The pages were onion-skin thin and dark from age, the writing made in brown ink. The script looked old, ancient even. And as she stared at the words, they began to move across the page, and she got a swimming feeling in her head.

Feeling suddenly light-headed, Jo she sat back down on her stool. Her hands began to shake, and she had a sinking feeling she knew what Pournelle had just *gifted* her with. Jo laid the book on the sparkling counter, and Pournelle poured her tea and fixed it exactly as she preferred.

"You just gave me a demon book—a demon *spell* book, if I'm not mistaken." The moving letters had cinched the notion that the book was demonic. Assumpta had once told her of a demon contract she'd tried to read. The letters and words swam around the page, making them impossible to understand. This book had to be of Hellish origin.

Pournelle nodded, pushing the tea toward her. "Drink."

"Is the book dangerous?"

He nodded again and fixed his own cup of tea.

"How is this supposed to help?" Jo implored. "I can't even read it."

"That's what these are for." Pournelle reached into his breast pocket and pulled out a small wooden box, polished to a high sheen, that looked like a tiny, impish coffin. It was hinged on one side and held a hasp on the other. There was no lock, but several scratches marred the smooth surface where one must once have been.

He pushed the box toward her.

CHAPTER 17

BEWARE OF GREEKS BEARING GIFTS..." JO muttered. She stared at the shiny, little box. It should comfort her that Pournelle had found a way for her to get information from the demon book—that he should even go out of his way to get her the book—but she didn't feel comforted. The vibe felt wrong. Something was off about the whole deal, but she'd be damned if she could figure out what it was.

"I beg your pardon?" Pournelle gave her an affronted look, eyebrows furrowed, lips settling into a thin, tight line.

She smiled. "Sorry. Greeks bearing gifts. You know, the Trojan war? Whatever's in that box is bound to be bad for me."

She flipped open the lid and was not surprised to see a pair of glasses. She hadn't known what kind to expect when she realized what must be in the box—something heavy and dull, thick-glassed, baroque and unwieldy, perhaps— but she was pleasantly surprised to see a dainty set of silver, filigreed spectacles that wouldn't cause a stir if she popped them on in the middle of a conversation with a customer.

She pulled them out of their wooden coffin—she couldn't quite get that image out of her head—unfolded the ear pieces and lifted them to her face.

"I should warn you," Pournelle said, gravely, "that using the glasses to read the book comes with a price."

"Of course it does," Jo said, not surprised at all. She wasn't dumb. She knew that whatever *demon-y* thing Pournelle offered must come with some kind of cost. The question was, was she willing to pay? *Hells, yes,* she thought, because at this point, the alternative was death.

"Wearing them will affect your sight."

Her heart stopped beating, and then started a double-tap tattoo in her chest. She lowered the glasses. "They'll make me go blind?"

Blindness was probably the one thing that would make her reconsider. *Who wants to be blind in a world full of color?* That almost made her sound petty. But having to live with blindness—when you're also aware of all the things that lurk in the dark? She shuddered, as a sudden chill crept up her neck. Maybe it was *because* she was attuned to the unseen, but in her case, she thought she'd rather be dead then blind. She'd probably die of a heart attack or something from living in a perpetual state of fear. And if her existence was all night all the time? *Hells, no.*

"Not at all." Pournelle brushed some imaginary dirt off his shoulder. Jo breathed a sigh of relief. "In fact, you will begin to see better. But you will also see things you most definitely will not want to see."

"But I can take the glasses off, *right?* And *not* see those things anymore?"

"I'm afraid that's not the way it works," Pournelle said. He stretched out his left arm and polished a jet-black cufflink. He seemed even more worried about his appearance, Jo thought. He was agitated about her having the book in her possession. *Why?*

Pournelle slammed his palm down on the counter in front of Jo and she jumped, startled. "Are you even listening to me?"

"Sorry. Just wandered off for a moment."

"Focus. I need you to understand this—understand the risks."

He was back to polishing the cufflink. "The glasses are meant to train new demons. Using them will *permanently* affect your normal vision. Essentially, you'll gain demon-sight. You'll see all the normal things on this plane, plus you'll see all the demonic things hiding here in plain sight."

"I put them on and—*bam!*—I can see what you see? And it's permanent?"

Giving her his full attention, Pournelle pursed his lips—a moue of distaste. "Yes—you put the glasses on and—*bam*—you'll have demon vision. But the permanence isn't immediate. It sets in after an accrual of use. You will start seeing some of the effects after you've used the glasses for the first time—assuming you use them for a few hours or so. The effects are cumulative. So, the longer you use them, the more you'll see. Eventually, your demon-vision will be permanent."

"And it's a foregone conclusion? As soon as I put the glasses on and look through them, it's only a matter of time before I'll have the sight?"

Pournelle sighed. He looked her in the eyes, holding her attention. "I suppose you could avoid gaining demon sight if you only put the glasses on for a few moments at a time—and only a few times. It's the continued use that does it. But frankly, even if you could avoid putting in the hours it might take you to read this book and find what you need—do you think you could? There's so much knowledge buried in this book—" He tapped the cover once with his index finger. "Do you think you could ignore that? *I* couldn't."

"I see."

"Not yet—but you will." Pournelle warmed his tea cup from the pot and dropped in another sugar cube. "It's not so bad, seeing what I see. You already dance on the edges of the paranormal, Jo. This simply allows you to see the things your mind already knows exist—at least as far as demons are concerned. You'll notice a few other things, too: ghosts, shades. After a while, you'll get used to the sight and tune them out."

She folded the glasses and tucked them back into the felt-lined box, closing the lid. "You're sure there's not another way? You really can't tell me what I need to know?"

He shook his head. "I only wish that it were so."

Would it be so bad? Seeing the things that Pournelle sees? Her fingers twitched, ready to pick up the glasses again. Her mind considered the possibilities, recalling a panoply of horror movies she'd seen growing up.

"How about if you read the book to me?" Jo balled her hand in a fist and dropped it to her side. She pushed the book toward him. "Then I wouldn't have to wear the glasses. I wouldn't have to pay any price."

Pournelle gave her a hungry look, as if reading the book was exactly what he wanted to do. There was a pause, a beat, when neither Jo nor Pournelle spoke. Then, he shook his head. "It doesn't work that way. The book isn't mine. Even though I can read demon script, I can't read it from this book since I don't own it."

"Why didn't you just keep your damned book? All of this would be moot!"

He gave her a pinched look and said quietly, "It wasn't my book to begin with."

Again, the silence stretched between them. Longer this time. He could *obtain* the book, but he couldn't read it, Jo thought. He could gift it to her, but he couldn't keep it. There was more to the story than he was saying, but she couldn't quite puzzle it out. One thing she knew for certain. "You stole it."

Pournelle nodded.

"Then how can you possibly gift it to me? The book wasn't yours to begin with."

"True enough." He looked almost sad at that admission. "But by demon law, a demon doesn't really own something if he doesn't have the power to keep it. Once I stole it, the book was effectively *ownerless*. I could do anything I wanted with it. So, I gave it to you. And, I've assured that you can't lose the book in any way. You *own* it now."

A pit opened in the center of her stomach as a chill washed over her. "Does that mean I'll have to fight off additional demons?" The last thing she needed to do was fight a war on two fronts. She didn't know if she had the strength to break the spell that weakened *her, that was killing her.* She didn't think she could do both.

"No. There's no way to trace where this book has gotten to. As far as the former owner is concerned, he's lost it."

With those words, and a baleful look at Jo, Pournelle raised his hand and snapped. He disappeared.

Jo stared at the book. She had the key to reading it, to discovering its secrets, but should she? Her fingers itched to turn the pages. She yearned to feel the cool, silver filigree resting on the bridge of her nose. It was almost an unquenchable urge to pull them both toward her and reveal the secrets that would make her well again.

She closed her eyes and took a deep breath, willing the sensation away. Was the book actually calling to her? Did it have some ability, some spell—or curse—that made her feel this compulsion to open the covers and look inside? Or maybe, it was just her own desire to make herself well, to feel better. Or maybe this irresistible impulse was just her own curiosity to know what the book contained.

She blew out her breath and opened her eyes. She wouldn't do it. Not right now. She refused to be compelled to do anything—even if it was something she wanted to do—if there was the smallest chance that there was something else urging her to do it. That urge, the pressure to open the book, might be concealing an ulterior motive. And if she was going to open herself up to the demon sight, she damn well wanted to do it on her own terms.

She reached for the little coffin-like box and laid it on top of the book, then tucked both beneath the counter—out of sight, out of mind, for the moment.

CHAPTER 18

THE NEXT MORNING, JUST AS JO WAS TURNING the *Closed* sign to *Open*, Assumpta arrived at The Turning Wheel. "You're here early." She stepped back and let Assumpta into the shop, bringing with her the odor of diesel fuel and exhaust from the cars and buses on their morning commute.

"I couldn't sleep after you sent the text last night. I can't wait to see what little *gift* Pournelle gave you this time." She waggled her eyebrows.

"It's not a gift!" Jo retrieved a cone of strawberry incense and her lighter from the high shelf by the door. She lit the incense, perhaps holding the tip of it in the flame a bit longer than necessary, while she gathered her thoughts. She blew on the end, watched the cherry flare a bright red, and then settled the cone in a brass dish on the same shelf.

"He *gave* you something. Ergo, it's a gift."

Jo gave Assumpta an exasperated look and walked around the back of the counter. "Okay, it's a gift—but not a *gift* gift." Assumpta just smiled. Jo lifted her mug. "Tea?"

"No, thanks. I've had a pot of coffee this morning while waiting to come on over. So, where is it?" She pulled a stool up to the counter, dropped her voluminous purse on the floor, and rested her elbows on the glass. "Show me."

Jo retrieved the book and the wooden box containing the glasses and laid them gently on the glass. She pushed them toward Assumpta.

"He gave you a book?" Assumpta lifted the wooden box aside and pulled the book toward her, running a finger over the gemstone in the cover.

"Not just any book—a *demon* book."

Assumpta looked up, held Jo's eye. When Jo just nodded, she looked down again, then opened the book about halfway through. "Yep, it's demon, all right. The letters are swimming all over the place." She looked away from the pages, closing the book, and blinked her eyes rapidly a few times.

"That's what these are for." Jo opened the small, coffin-like box and pulled out the glasses. She unfolded the ear pieces and handed them to Assumpta. "Don't put them on. Don't look through the glass."

"Don't put them on?"

Jo explained how the glasses worked while Assumpta admired the detail of the frames.

"It's a shame," Assumpta said, running a finger along the filigreed ear piece. "They're really quite lovely. But you can't wear them. You have to find another way to read this book. Maybe you can persuade Pournelle to read it for you." She folded the glasses and put them back in their box.

"I asked him to do that," Jo said. "He said he *can't* read the book since he doesn't own it."

"Then give the book to him. Problem solved."

Jo hadn't thought of that, but just considering it made her rueful. "Do you realize what I'd be giving up if I did that?"

"Yeah—the ability to see creepy-crawly stuff all the time. Trust me, you don't want to see what hides in the shadows in broad daylight."

That gave Jo pause. "You say that as if you know what you're talking about." She gave Assumpta a hard look. "Do *you* have the demon sight?" If so, what else had her friend *not* been telling her?

"God, no!" Assumpta ran a hand through her tousled curls. "Pournelle once..." She mumbled the rest of the words and Jo couldn't hear them clearly.

"Pournelle what?" Jo demanded.

Assumpta blushed. "He once shared his demon sight with me."

"And you're freaked out because he gave me *a gift?*"

"A gift is more intimate than sharing demon sight—it was only for a few seconds!"

"Not. This. Kind. Of. Gift." Jo punctuated each word with her pointed finger, striking the demon book each time she uttered a syllable. She gritted her teeth. "What is the sight like?"

"Bright." Assumpta paused to think about it. "Clear. Precise. Everything comes into sharp focus."

"That's it?"

"I don't want to glorify it."

It didn't sound so bad at all. "What about...evil things?"

Assumpta shrugged. "I saw a pair of ghosts and a demon in its true form. Maybe a vampire. I couldn't be certain—and I never had a chance to confirm it with Pournelle."

"That's it?"

"I experienced the sight for a less than a minute—it probably wasn't long enough for me to see other things."

"Would it be so bad? We both already know what lurks in the shadows." Jo felt a tiny bit ashamed of the whining note in her voice. Who was she trying to convince—Assumpta or herself?

Assumpta pushed the book back toward Jo. "But we don't need to *see* the horrors or be reminded of them all the time. What kind of life would that be like?"

"Balanced?"

"How do you figure?"

"Well—" Jo sat on the stool behind the counter and sipped her tea. "We see the light now, seeing the dark might give me a different perspective. Show me where to be more cautious, when to lay new wards. Maybe I'll be able to protect myself more."

"Maybe it would drive you insane." Assumpta brushed a wayward strand of hair out of her face. "But you're crazy if you think having

117

demon sight would make things balanced. It would be just the opposite, making things unbalanced. You'd only begin to see more evil. What kind of person would that make you?"

Jo ignored the last question. "Why do you think it would be unbalanced?"

"It just is. You don't have *angelic* sight or *holy* sight now. You don't see the glorious things watching over you in your life. Why invite the darkness when you won't invite the light?"

Jo pushed away from the counter, away from Assumpta, leaning back so far as to almost unbalance herself.

"*Angelic* sight?" Was there even such a thing? She felt almost sucker-punched by Assumpta. "Are you implying that I need to give up paganism and join the ranks of Christians—of Catholics?"

"No! I—" Assumpta faltered a moment, then, "No, I wasn't implying it at all. But maybe you should consider it, especially if—"

"You're as bad as Father Tony."

"As bad as? I thought you liked him and didn't mind that he suggested you come to church."

"That was before I thought the two of you might be ganging up on me."

Assumpta straightened. "We're not ganging up on you. I simply meant that if you're going to get involved with darkness, you might want to get involved with light."

"And Christianity is the only way to do that?"

"No, it's not the only way. You're not hearing me." Assumpta stood. "Maybe I should come back another time?"

"Yeah—" Jo nodded her head. "That would probably be best."

"Promise me you won't put on the glasses," Assumpta said. "Promise me you'll look for another way to figure this out."

"Because you care so much about me?"

"I do."

"Wearing the glasses is the fastest way to obtain the information I need to cure this curse. I might die before I figure it out."

"Not with Pournelle's scarab. Promise me."

Reluctantly, Jo pushed the glasses and the demon book aside. She nodded. "For now. But I won't put this off forever."

"You won't have to. While you're looking for answers in your way, I'll look in mine."

"With your *Christian* pendulum?"

"I've got to go," Assumpta said, curtly. "I've got class at one." She picked up her purse and walked out the door.

Jo reached for the rosemary teapot on top of the samovar Pournelle had left behind. She needed another bracing cup of tea. That was the first time she'd ever had a fight with Assumpta. It hadn't been pleasant. Neither would losing her friendship. But if Assumpta didn't come around, so be it.

CHAPTER 19

AFTER ASSUMPTA LEFT, JO PULLED HER NOTEBOOK down off the shelf and opened it to a fresh page. She flipped up the lid of the wooden box and removed the demon glasses, giving them a thorough examination. They really were pretty—aged silver with a soft shine, not the garish gleam of chrome, nickel, or silver plate. The delicate filigree detail appeared ultra-feminine until she looked closer and noticed that the tiny swirls and delicate wiring created dancing skulls instead of flourishing roses along the ear pieces. Jo grinned. It was just the kind of thing she loved.

She stepped from behind the counter and over to a rotating display of necklaces, on which was attached a mirror. She held the glasses in front of her face, not staring through them, but simply getting an idea of how they might look on her.

Old fashioned, but flattering. If she attached a retro chain, they'd be the perfect accessory—and guaranteed not to get lost or casually picked up by anyone who might walk into the store.

Should she do it? Put on the glasses and gain the ability of demon sight? She'd know *immediately* if a demon walked into her store and see its true form. She'd be able to read the demon book and fix whatever ailed her. She could protect Assumpta, the rest of her friends, their families—everyone the demons said they would come after.

She could *use* demon magic—for good, of course. The guide was thick with at least a thousand pages of spells and lore, and who knew what other helpful information?

But then she could no longer pretend that ghosts didn't exist in this part of Baltimore, that they didn't waltz through her house on occasion. She'd be able to *see* it happening—instead of just assuming. And she'd see other monsters, other *things,* she probably had no name for—and gain information she'd probably feel safer not knowing.

There was comfort in ignorance. Could she give that up?

It's not like she could read the guide for a few hours—find out what she needed—and then halt the process by never touching it, or the glasses, ever again. There was too much knowledge there—too much power—to ignore it forever. She wouldn't have the willpower to stay away from it. Pournelle was right. Offered the chance to gain a certain bit of power against the dark side, she had no choice but to accept it.

The book had already accepted her, why shouldn't she embrace all that came with it?

Still, she wavered. There were so many good things that could come from this—and so many bad ones.

Her cell phone rang. Jo reached into her pocket and looked at the screen. *Assumpta.* She slid her finger across the screen and answered. "Hey. What's—"

"My cousin Sheila is really, really sick. She's got a raging fever, and she's lethargic, and—" Assumpta's voice was thick with tears.

"Oh, no. What's going on?" Jo asked, almost certain she knew the answer. She felt herself nodding at Assumpta's reply.

"Hugh almost couldn't wake her this morning! They've cut short their honeymoon." Assumpta's voice rose to a high pitch of anxiety. "The ambulance is taking her to the hospital now."

"It could be a coincidence," Jo said, knowing instinctively that it wasn't, and regretting her words the moment she'd uttered them. There just weren't words to comfort people in situations like this. Assumpta couldn't be comforted. "I'm working on something. "I think I know what to do."

"Don't bother. I'm going to give the medallion to Pournelle." The tears were gone, Assumpta's voice was evenly pitched and strong. She'd made her mind up.

"No!" Jo felt her own panic rising. Giving the medallion over wouldn't do any good. Surely Assumpta understood that. "If you're doing this because of our argument—"

"I'm not." Assumpta took a deep, tremulous breath. She'd contained the tears, but they were still evident in her voice. "Water under the bridge. I know you didn't mean the accusations, just like you know I'd never suggest that Christianity is the answer to everything."

Jo nodded along to Assumpta's words, in complete agreement. "I'm sorry—"

"Me, too. Now, I'm going to give the medallion to the demons. It solves all our problems." Her voice got stronger. "Once they have it, they'll break the spell. You'll no longer be dying. They'll stop coming after my family. They'll stop coming after *you*." Assumpta sniffled, and the tears were back. "*Everyone* will be fine."

"We don't know that, Assumpta." She couldn't let Assumpta give up the medallion. There were no guarantees with demons. And if Assumpta were thinking clearly instead of worried for her cousin, she would realize that herself. "The demons' threats didn't imply that they'll stop any evil they've already instigated. You might hand it over, and they could leave the death spell in place. Hells! You know what liars they are. They might accept the medallion and kill us all anyway."

"I've got to try."

"Wait—" Jo remembered her visit from Mars—Saint Michael— just before she had been rushed to the hospital. She'd meant to tell Assumpta the last time they'd gotten together, but Assumpta had stormed out before she had a chance. "There's something I've been meaning to tell you…" She told Assumpta about Mars' visit, and his message to Assumpta that refusing to give him the medallion was not a sin *in extremis*. "You can make things right if you get it to him soon."

Assumpta sniffed and swallowed hard. "I can't. I'm going to give it to Pournelle."

"Then Pournelle will realize that you've had it all along. He might hate you."

"As if I care for the friendship of a demon."

You do care, Jo thought, *and you'll regret it if you lose it*. But she couldn't say that out loud. Assumpta was definitely not in a receptive mood. "Just give me a few days or so. If I can't figure something else out before then, you can present the medallion to Pournelle."

"Sheila might not have a few days."

"Two, then. I promise you I'll figure something out." She looked down at the filigree glasses, clutched in her left hand, knowing she'd made her decision. And then she made another. "Come get my scarab. Give it to Sheila."

"And then you'll be dying again. Who will save Sheila?"

"Then call Pournelle. Ask him for another scarab. *Do not* tell him about the medallion." Jo rubbed her forehead where an ache was starting to settle. "Buy me some time."

"Two days. No more. And then we've got to consider giving the demons what they want."

"I'll get to work," Jo said. "I'll call you when I know more." She cut the line before Assumpta could answer—or question what she might do. Decision made, she slid the phone back into her pocket and turned back to the mirrored stand. Jo settled the glasses on the bridge of her nose—they fit perfectly—and looked into the mirror.

Everything came into crisp focus, and brightened, as if an overhead light had been switched on. She could see each pore on her face with amazing clarity, and the wispy hairs of her brows, all different shades of brown where normally she only noticed one shade. Even her eyes looked different. She saw glints of a golden pigmentation in the brown.

Jo looked around the store. Even ten feet away, she noticed the detail of the individual barbs of the feathers on the delicate fairies hanging from the ceiling, and further away she could almost—*almost*—read the labels on the herb packaging.

She focused on the packaging, and the writing came into view.

Amazing. Had her eyes been playing tricks on her because she was tired? She had only needed to concentrate until they focused? Or was that a demon-glasses trick? She looked to the back of the store, where she could see the yellow stickers on the clearance items, but certainly not the prices written on them. She focused on the sticker, blinked rapidly a few times, and the tiny numbers in her own handwriting came into view. She could read the sale prices perfectly. It was definitely the glasses.

These could be addictive, she thought, enjoying the improved vision. It wasn't like she couldn't see well before—she could just see so much better now. She imagined her vision with the glasses might be compared to how an owl, or an eagle, might see. *How useful they could be in the store! Anywhere!*

Her smile faded. "That's just the kind of thinking I need to avoid," she whispered to herself. "I'll only use them long enough to find out what I need, and then take them off. The less demon stuff I see, the happier I'll be." She shivered. "I can't imagine how scary demon vision would be on a permanent basis."

And her heart sunk, because she knew it was already too late.

She took a deep breath to bolster herself, returned to the counter and opened the demon book, looking for a table of contents. The pages were so thin, she could see the shadow of the writing on the reverse side bleeding through. She fanned the pages again with her thumb. There was no table of contents in the front of the book. *Damn.* She turned to the back, hoping for an index. None there, as well.

"Well, how am I supposed to find the spell I need?"

She turned back to the front of the book. "'*Begin at the beginning*,'" she said, quoting the King of Hearts from *Alice in Wonderland*, "'*and go on till you come to the end: then stop.*' Or at least go on until I find what I'm looking for," Jo said. "Looks like I'm here for the long haul."

She slid the glasses to the top of her head—blinking as the light dimmed all around her and her normal vision returned. She pushed the book away, got a fresh mug from under the counter, and held it under the samovar's spout and pulled the lever. Piping hot water poured into her cup. She added a ginger peach tea bag from her stash and breathed in the sharp aroma of spice. She smiled. Pournelle had left behind the magic samovar and tea pot! Her favorite black tea always fresh and ready in the pot, and perfectly hot water always available from the samovar when she was in the mood for something else. She wasn't giving it up. Not if she didn't have to.

Fortified with tea and a seat to make herself comfortable, she pulled the book closer and turned to the first page. Unusual letters twirled and danced across the paper—then she remembered to put the glasses back on. Once she did, everything came into bright, sharp focus, and the letters ceased their waltzing

Across the top of the first page, in bold letters, were the words, *To Improve Hearing.* Below it was a list of spell ingredients: A copper bowl, a hematite knife, fire, halite— *rock salt,* Jo translated—field mouse ears, field mouse blood. That's where she stopped reading and turned the page.

To Call Vermin, was the spell on the next page. *Why would you want to call vermin?* she wondered. To get field mice ears, to improve your hearing, she thought. The required ingredients list was much longer. Like the first, it started with the hardware necessary—a glass bowl, a hematite knife—and moved on to the actual spell components, this one requiring roach legs, bat wings and rat tails. The written instructions took two pages, so she skipped ahead to the next page and read the spell's title: *To Find Money.* The ingredients seemed simple enough. She read a few lines of the spell. It seemed straightforward.

That one might be interesting, she thought, but for another time. *"Concentrate," she muttered.*

Something across the room caught her eye. One of the fairies hanging from the ceiling was rocking gently, as if caught in a breeze. But the front door hadn't opened—the usual cause of any swaying among the fairy and dragon armada. She hadn't walked across the room, brushed against it. And she was alone. At least, she thought she was alone.

Her heart started gently thumping—just hard enough to let her know it had gotten a little bit of a jumpstart. She scanned the room. Even with the glasses, she didn't see anything amiss. She listened hard for a few moments, continued to look around the room, but didn't see anything. Little by little, she relaxed, and returned her attention to the book. It must have been her imagination.

Jo sighed, sipped her tea, and flipped a few pages, just reading the titles of the spells. They were a motley lot: *To Cause an Itch, To Gain a Friend, To Cause Warts*—that one made her giggle. She knew a few people she'd like to give warts to.

She sobered when she turned to the next page. *To Kill by Fire*. It wasn't quite what she was looking for, but it was close. She needed to find something along the lines of *To Kill by Disease*, or *To Kill by Illness*, right? She flipped again. *To Shapechange*. She turned to the next page. *To Cause Injury by Falling*. And the next. *To Find a Lost Love*.

"This is useless!" she shouted, flipping to the next page, then flipping it again when it wasn't what she wanted. There seemed to be no order or pattern to how the spells were laid out in the book. "How the hell am I supposed to find the spell I need without reading this damned book from beginning to end?" She turned a few more pages. "All I need is the spell which kills by disease."

The book was ripped from Jo's hands by some unseen force and slammed closed on the counter top. Just as suddenly, the book slammed opened flat and the pages began turning, slowly at first, then picking up momentum, turning and turning and turning, as if whipped by a strong wind. A moment later, the book lay open before her, still as death, the spell *To Kill by Malady*, written across the top of the page.

Heart galloping, Jo stared at the book.

Her cell phone rang, and she jumped. It was Assumpta. "Pournelle doesn't have another scarab," she said, "but he's got a temporary solution for Sheila."

"That's great." Jo stared at the book, wondering if it would move again. "I've made some progress here."

"You've found the cure?"

"Not yet. But soon. I'm certain." The book remained motionless.

"He doesn't have the means to help anyone else." Assumpta was weepy again, and Jo felt the anguish deep in her own gut.

"He won't need to. I promise—" Jo hoped she wouldn't have to break that promise. "Now let me get back to work." She ended the call.

CHAPTER 20

JO REACHED FOR THE BOOK, THEN PULLED HER hand back, suddenly unwilling to touch it. Then she laughed. Why was she so afraid of a book? The book could do her no harm— even if it was demonic in nature.

And apparently, one needed only to ask it for a spell, and it would find it for you. No wonder it had no contents or index. If only her other books would be so accommodating!

She tested her theory, making certain it was no fluke. "I need to find the demons who cast the malady spell on me."

The book slammed shut again, and Jo jumped. She stepped back away from the counter as the book opened again and pages began to turn of their own accord. Faster and faster they whipped, stopping suddenly about a quarter way through the book. *To Find Your Enemy*, was written across the top of the page. A long list of spell components followed, and it included a complicated spell casting ritual, as well. Her heart sank.

Then it dawned on her that she didn't need to know *where* her enemy was—and she didn't need to know *what* spell had been cast. She only needed to counter or reverse it. *Sheila and I will be cured*, she thought. And then she could get down to the business of taking care of the demons who'd cast the spell. Maybe she'd give them warts—no, hemorrhoids—

or something *both* humiliating and painful. She chuckled at her own revenge. But seriously, if she could trap the demons in Hell—their power halved, according to Pournelle—then they couldn't hurt anyone anymore.

So, she would counter the death spell, then send the demons back to Hell.

She said, "I need the counter-spell for the malady one."

Jo was ready for the slam of the book this time. It re-opened and turned pages until it neared the end of the book. When the pages finally came to rest, Jo pulled the book closer to her and read, "*To Counter a Death Spell.* Ingredients: A brass pot, a steel knife, purified water, halite, rosemary, *dämota freathoph serte.*" The last ingredient hadn't translated into English like the rest of the spell had. She had a feeling it was written in a language other than *demon. Was that why it wouldn't translate?*

The first part—*dämota*—was pretty easy to figure out—she needed something demon-related, or something that belonged to a demon. The rest of the phrase made no sense to her, but she knew who she could ask the next time she saw him.

Or, I could just summon him, Jo thought, punching the button on the cash register which opened the drawer. It flew open with a *ding!* and she selected Pournelle's calling card, sliding a finger along one edge of it. She stared at it a few moments, trying to decide if now were a good time to call him.

The shop bell rang and the door opened. Jo pulled the glasses off. At once, the light in the store appeared to dim, and her vision, which she once thought perfect, seemed to grow fuzzy. One of her regulars walked in, Chip—a cheerful young man who attended the local college. Jo smiled and waved. "Can I help you with anything?"

"Just browsing today," he said, smiling. "I've got some time to kill before classes."

Jo nodded, and he made his way to the rear of the store where the books—and clearance items—were. "Okay. Just let me know."

She used Pournelle's card as a bookmark, then stowed the demon book beneath the counter, and placed the glasses in their wooden box, ready to hide them, too. Then, she had second thoughts about putting them away. She could use them, couldn't she, to keep better watch on the store? She'd never had a reason to suspect the young man of shoplifting, but it would be fun to be able to see what he perused from this distance. Maybe she could turn her browser into a buyer by offering him a discount on something he touched. *Oh, you're interested in the dousing wands? They're 15% off today.*

She was smiling as she retrieved the glasses and donned them. She blinked at the sudden brightness and turned toward the young man, now standing in front of the cauldrons.

As she watched, the glamour of the young man faded and a demon stood in his place.

The smile slid off Jo's face. It took every ounce of courage she had not to gasp aloud. Her *regular* was a demon, the *worst* kind, she knew, since it matched the description Assumpta had once given her. Its skin was mottled black and red, wrinkled heavily around the neck and its broad, muscled shoulders. Giant, leathery wings, folded on its back, dragged on the floor, and long, curled horns—like a ram's—protruded from its forehead.

It raised a taloned hand and tapped a claw against an enamel cauldron.

Jo pulled the glasses from her face, folded the ear pieces, and set them gingerly on the counter. The room dimmed, and her customer was once again a young man with shaggy blond hair and smooth, dimpled cheeks. She touched the scarab at her neck, wondering if she should offer up a quick prayer to Mars—just in case he'd actually come to visit. She'd never been the praying type. Wouldn't Mars expect a tribute? What could she sacrifice? Would it be enough in this moment to save her if the demon decided to harm her?

Probably not. The only person she could depend on right now was herself.

But this demon had been in her store many times in the past, and it had never hurt her. Why would it do anything to her this time? She had no reason to believe that it would.

She took a few silent, deep breaths, willing herself to a calmer state, and opened her inventory book—something mundane to keep her mind occupied while there was a *customer* in the store. How many more of her regulars were demons? Or something else?

An antsy fifteen minutes later, the demon purchased some musk-scented incense and left. Jo sighed with relief. It couldn't be all bad, right? It had actually purchased something. Maybe, it was just trying to fit in.

"And maybe," she mused aloud, "it's been watching me all this time and reporting back to the others." She tried to think back to the last time she saw him and how frequently he'd come around. She couldn't remember. *That was a good thing, right?* Frustrated, she made a fist and pounded it on the cash register, then took another deep breath to calm herself.

Jo retrieved the demon book from under the counter and once more donned the glasses. She blinked away the brightness while she made room on the counter for the book to do its work. She couldn't heal herself yet—not without *dämota freathoph serte*, so she'd start with finding a spell to banish the demons who'd bespelled her and Sheila. "Show me a spell to send demons back to Hell."

Immediately, the book slammed open and pages began turning. A moment later, it came to rest open again on the spell Jo wanted. She started jotting down the necessary ingredients, many of which she had in the store—or her own kitchen. But there was one ingredient she didn't have: the blood of a demon.

She slammed the book closed herself. *How in the nine Hells am I supposed to obtain demon blood?* To make matters worse, the spell required that the demons be present when she worked the spell. *Well, damn*, she thought. *That's a complication I don't need.*

Jo pulled off the glasses and rubbed her eyes. Things weren't as dim, or as fuzzy, as she thought they might be. She put the glasses back on. The room got brighter, but not so much as when she first started wearing the glasses.

It looked like it wouldn't take as long as Pournelle thought for full-blown demon-vision to kick in. It was already happening.

CHAPTER 21

LATER THAT EVENING, JO AND ASSUMPTA SAT AT the glass counter in the store, sipping tea from the teapot above the small samovar Pournelle had left, and discussing strategies for getting rid of unwanted demons. Jo held the demon book open, reading a list of spell components aloud from it. The edges of the thin pages tickled her finger tips as she turned them. With each flip of the page, the aroma of *old book*—and something akin to moist dirt— teased her, like a half-remembered memory.

The bell rang as the door was pushed open, and Pournelle walked in.

"Speak of the devil," Assumpta said, and looked at Jo, her lips twitching.

Simultaneously, they both burst out laughing.

"Not funny." Pournelle frowned and brushed imaginary lint from his sleeve. He was especially dapper tonight in navy pinstripes and Italian leather shoes.

"Says you," Jo said, winking at Assumpta. "Care to join us for tea?" She lifted the teapot from the top of the samovar and poured a cup for Pournelle. The aroma of black tea filled the air.

"In some circles, your joke is tantamount to a *promotion*. It could get me killed for reaching above my station." That sobered the women.

He grabbed a stool from just inside the store room and placed it next to Assumpta's, joining them at the counter. He accepted the teacup from Jo, breathing in the fragrant steam before taking a sip. "Enjoying my little gift, are you?"

"I can keep it?" Jo's eyes lit up.

"Indeed." Pournelle set the cup down and added lemon and sugar from a small dish beside the samovar. "But you're still brewing pekoe? I admit it's my favorite."

Jo's eyes lit up. "I can brew other tea? How do I empty the pot?" She lifted her cup and drained it in one swallow. "I'm ready for another."

It was Pournelle's turn to smile. "I thought you would have figured that out by now." He nodded to the demon book. "Have you learned how to use the demon guide?"

Jo pulled the book toward her. "Yes—by accident. I got so frustrated I yelled at the damned thing."

Pournelle chuckled.

"*Damned* thing...pun intended?" Assumpta asked. Pournelle and Jo groaned. Then, Jo smiled.

"I think I know what Pournelle is getting at. The pot works like the book." She turned to the samovar and tapped the China teapot on top. "Golden monkey tea."

"Another black tea!" Pournelle said, smiling.

"I know." Jo shrugged. "But I've always wanted to try it." She found a clean mug under the counter, poured herself a cup, and took a sip. Fragrant and earthy, but she couldn't quite taste the peach notes the tea was famous for. "I love how tea from this pot is always the perfect temperature. Thank you."

Pournelle nodded. "How's the golden monkey?"

"A little strong, I think."

"Try this." Pournelle took the cup from her and diluted the brew with piping hot water from the spout on the samovar. "Like the tea, the hot water will never run out."

"The gift that keeps on giving." Jo took the cup back, sipped, and nodded, enjoying it much more upon tasting the peach. "It's perfect."

"But you didn't come here to drink tea," Assumpta ventured. "Have you heard anything?"

"No." He looked wistful. "Lips are surprisingly tight down in Hell these days, but I'll keep listening."

"Really?" Assumpta sipped her tea, drawing out the moment. "I'd have thought with your connections you'd have heard something by now."

Pournelle's face lost all expression, and he turned blank eyes on Assumpta. It scared Jo—just a bit. Her heart beat a little faster in her chest. It was like the return of the old Pournelle, the demon who existed to torment Assumpta before they'd made their pact of *good will* toward each other. His voice clipped, he said, "I don't think you know as much about my *connections* as you think you do, Ms. O'Connor. I'll thank you to trust me, not *push* me, on the issue." And then his face lost its blankness. He stretched out a hand and fingered the spine of the demon spell book, stroking it once. His expression interested, he asked Jo in a much friendlier voice, "How is the studying going?"

Jo smiled tightly. Was she wrong to be worried that Pournelle's coldness a moment ago meant that he could turn on them at any moment? She took a deep breath and let it out quickly. There was no reason to think he might turn. He was simply expressing his anger—very controlled anger—like anyone would do when being needled about something. Her smile softened into something more genuine. "I'm glad you asked. There's something I need to run by you." She picked up her notes on the *counter* spell. "To break the death curse upon Sheila and me, I need something called *dämota freathoph serte*." She knew she killed the pronunciation.

"Do you mean, *dämota freathoph serte*?" He pronounced the second word as three syllables, with emphasis on *topf*.

"Yes. The glasses wouldn't translate the words."

"I think because it's not the demon language." Pournelle lifted his mug of tea and breathed in the steam.

"I assumed as much," Jo said. "Do you know what it means?"

He sipped from his mug, looking over the rim and locking his eyes with hers. "It's a bastardization of ancient Latin. What you need, my dear, is some dead man's blood." He sipped again.

"Dead man's blood?" Well, she'd been wrong about *dämota meaning something demon. But what is it with demons and the use of blood in their spells?* She offered Pournelle a wry look. "Short of killing someone, or hanging out at the local morgue—which I'm certain would involve a felony or two—how do you suggest I obtain it?"

"You mustn't take things so literally, my dear." Pournelle set his mug down and straightened the silver cuff link on his left wrist. "Demons are rarely literal. Have you heard the term *dead man walking?*"

"A prisoner on death row," Assumpta said. "Still alive, but death is a foregone conclusion."

Pournelle nodded.

"And how do you expect me to get blood from death row inmates?" Jo asked. "Are you going to take me there? Can you draw blood? Because I sure as hell can't."

"I'm suggesting nothing of the sort." Pournelle looked at her expectantly, and she felt her frustration level rise. Her face grew hot with anger.

Jo opened her mouth to respond with something smart, when Assumpta laid a calming hand on her wrist. "He doesn't have to take you anywhere," she said. "Pournelle is referring to you. *You* are the dead man walking."

There was a brief silence in the room while Jo collected her thoughts. *Don't be so literal,* Pournelle had told her. Of course. Why hadn't she seen that right away?

Pournelle gave his attention to his right cuff link. "The alternative, of course, is to kill the demons who cast the spell. Killing them severs the magical link between you."

"Link?"

Pournelle nodded, his face grave. "The spell creates a magical bond between you and the demons who cast it. The bond acts as a siphon, funneling your life force to the demons. As you weaken and die, the demons gain in strength. Kill those responsible for the spell and you cut the tie that binds you together."

"But is there time to arrange a confrontation with the demons? Would that be faster than casting the counter-spell?"

Pournelle shook his head. "Moot question, really. As soon as the demons figure out you've cast the counter spell, they'll come to you and try to kill you."

"That wasn't mentioned in the book!"

"Because it's a demon book. And demons know the nature of other demons. The warning isn't necessary."

"So…I cast the counter spell and *boom!* the demons arrive and try to kill me?"

"It doesn't happen that fast. The bond is severed, but it might take them a day or so to realize they're no longer gaining power from you. Before you cast the counter-spell, be certain you're willing and able to confront those demons."

"I don't see that I have a choice." Jo set her mug on the counter and pushed it away from her. "Not if I want to help Sheila, or the next family member they decide to cast the death spell on."

Pournelle nodded grimly. "Sheila will need protection, too."

Assumpta set her mug on the counter. "Can you help with that?"

"I'll do what I can." He stood and looked at Jo. "Take the scarab off before you collect your blood," he said. "As long as you're wearing it, you're *not* dying and any blood you collect won't be good for the spell. You might consider bottling up a pint or two while you're at it. It'll keep—and you may never get this chance again—I hope."

He snapped his fingers and was gone. Three narrow bottles made of brown, wavy glass, sat on the stool in his place.

CHAPTER 22

ASSUMPTA LIFTED THE BOTTLES FROM THE STOOL and set them atop the glass counter in front of Jo, the dark glass clanking discordantly. Jo shoved aside the demon book and lifted one of the bottles. "Heavy," she said, pushing one of the other bottles toward Assumpta so she could examine it more closely. "They're old, I think. I wonder if there's anything special about them."

"I assume they're magical in some way—*demon* magical." Assumpta pulled the glass stopper out of her bottle and sniffed. "They seem clean, at least. Do you want me to consult the pendulum about them?" She reached for her voluminous purse.

"Nah. Too much effort." Jo pulled the heavy glass stopper from one and lifted it to her nose. The air inside seemed cool and without fragrance, except perhaps *clean glass*. She set it down on the counter. "I don't think we need to do any magic to figure out what these things do. Collect some blood in them, and the blood will likely remain fresh for quite some time—if not forever. It's just the kind of thing Pournelle would have access to."

Assumpta was nodding. She stoppered the bottle and pushed it back toward the others. "You're really going to do this?"

"Like I told Pournelle, I don't think I have a choice."

Assumpta looked at the three bottles. "But it's an awful lot of blood."

"I don't know," Jo said. "The bottles are thick glass. They can't hold more than a few ounces each—a cup at the most. And I don't even need that much for the spell. But like Pournelle suggested, I might as well collect more than I need and save some for later."

"But how are you going to do it? It's going to be really messy."

"I've got that covered, I think." Jo reached for her phone and sent a quick text. "One of the women who comes to my Thursday night class is a nursing student. We've gotten friendly. I'm going to ask her to bring me a collection needle."

Assumpta raised her eyebrows. "Do you think she will? Maybe she'll help you gather the blood."

"I wouldn't ask Julie to do that."

"But you'll ask her to bring you a needle?"

"Sure," Jo said. "I'll tell her I need it for an herbology project or something. I don't want to freak her out by asking her to draw my blood—especially blood I want to store in these bottles."

Assumpta fingered the stopper of the bottle closest to her. "You know, you really don't have to do this. You have the scarab to keep you safe."

"Sheila doesn't—and there's the threat of the demons attacking more of your family and friends. I can't ignore that."

"Thank you." She was silent for a moment. "What about the demons who will come after you?"

"I have some ideas—most of which consist of us going on the offensive—instead of sitting back and waiting. I'll consult the book for something concrete. Tonight, I'll collect the blood."

CHAPTER 23

JO CLOSED THE STORE, AND SET A FEW EXTRA wards around the door and windows, then went upstairs to her apartment. She checked the wards in there, too, making certain all were in order before she sat down to draw blood. She wanted no interruptions.

Once assured, she sat cross-legged on the floor in front of the fireplace, a small fire burning brightly in the hearth. She wanted to be comfortable while she drew her own blood and, at the same time, be careful. She sat on a plastic tarp—an old shower curtain—in case she spilled any blood; she was low to the floor in case she passed out, which she did *not* anticipate happening; and she was in front of the fire to keep herself warm through the process. Her cell phone and her notebook were within easy reach on the floor to her right. She was ready to begin.

Jo took off the scarab necklace and set it on the coffee table in front of her. She felt no adverse effects—which surprised her. She thought she might have felt a bout of nausea or weakness, but was glad when neither occurred. Sticking a needle in her arm would take all the concentration she could muster.

The needle her friend Julie had given her was attached to a narrow flexible hose with a plastic mechanism on the bottom meant to be inserted into a small vacuum test tube to collect blood cleanly and without spillage. Julie hadn't brought any vacuum tubes, she said, because she didn't want to tempt Jo into actually trying to collect her own blood. "This was about herbology research, right?" Julie had asked.

Jo had nodded and said all the right things. What Julie didn't know wouldn't hurt her. The only problem was, where to stick herself? The vein by her elbow was the most obvious choice, but she wasn't certain she could actually find the vein there. She'd squeezed her fist and held it, and tapped on the blue line she saw there, but nothing looked large enough to stick a needle into. And even though the needles were made to facilitate one-handed insertion, she didn't consider that a bonus with her total lack of experience. She needed to stick herself someplace easy.

"Hand it is," she muttered, looking at the veins that were slightly raised on the back of her hand. At least she knew she'd be hitting the right spot—if not a great spot.

She unstoppered the first bottle and placed it near her left knee, then opened the sterile packaging of the needle. She pulled the needle assembly from the package and cut off the locking mechanism with a pair of scissors, which left her with the needle attached to the very thin hose. *Perfect.* She could shove the needle into her vein and the end of the hose into the bottle, and it would be almost as clean as having a vacuum tube to work with. Only now, she could collect three bottles full of blood—she guessed about a little more than a pint's worth—instead of an ounce or two in various medical test tubes.

She only needed about an ounce for the demon spell. Maybe she should be content to fill only one bottle and save the others for something else. Then she remembered the conversation with Pournelle: when would she ever get another chance to obtain *dead man's blood?* Three bottles it was.

With thumb and forefinger, Jo grasped the plastic wings which served as handles on the collection needle, pressed it against the vein on the top of her hand and pushed. The needle skidded across her skin, drawing blood, but not entering the vein. She'd only scratched across the surface of her hand. Red droplets of blood welled in the scratch, some larger than others. "What a waste," she muttered.

She didn't want to set the needle down and possibly contaminate it in order to wipe the blood, so she tried again, pushing against the skin a little more firmly with the point of the needle.

The needle slipped on the blood and again skidded across her hand, scratching it more deeply, and drawing more blood, since Jo had applied more pressure.

"Hells' bells," she cursed, fighting the urge to alleviate the pain by rubbing the scratch. Instead, she took a deep breath and let it out slowly, watching more blood droplets form on the surface of her hand, and lamenting the loss of every one of them. Each drop was one less in the bottle.

She had to be able to do this. Nurses made it look so damned easy. What was she doing wrong? She thought back to a few weeks ago when she had to have blood drawn. And then it dawned on her. *Angle.*

Once more, she placed the needle on the top of her hand by the vein, this time tilting it at a much steeper angle, as if she would push the needle through her hand instead of trying to horizontally pierce through the vein. With steady pressure, she broke through her skin—which hurt much less than the scratch she'd given herself. She pushed again, sliding the steel point more deeply into her hand and into the vein.

Blood appeared in the tiny hose.

Yes!

She released the plastic wings to rest against the top of her hand, stabilizing the needle. The blood flowed a little faster. So, she quickly tucked the end of the tiny hose into the top of the bottle with her free hand, and rested the needled hand on her knee, careful not to jar it.

Then she relaxed against the couch, letting her head fall back on the seat cushion, and closed her eyes. She let the warmth of the fire permeate her and willed the scratches on the top of her hand to stop throbbing.

Jo thought she would take some notes while she did this, but she suddenly found herself too fatigued to do so. She'd do it in the morning, when she was fresh from sleep.

After a few moments, she opened her eyes and checked the bottle, having to lift both it and her hand upward to cast enough light through the glass to see the blood level. The bottle was nearly full. She transferred the hose to the second bottle, then stoppered the first and leaned forward to place it on the coffee table where she couldn't accidentally knock it over.

"One down, two to go," Jo said, shivering with a sudden chill. She reached for an afghan on the arm of the loveseat behind her and spread it half over her shoulders and half over the part of her lap and arm that wasn't attached to a needle. Even with the fire, she was starting to get cold. Her hands and feet were freezing. A few moments later, her teeth began to chatter.

She carefully lifted the second bottle against the light to check the contents. Three-quarters full. Was the second bottle filling more slowly? She pulled the hose up out of the bottle to watch the blood drain. It was hard to tell, because the hose was so thin, but it didn't look like the blood had slowed. She hoped she didn't have to worry about that.

A few moments later, the bottle was nearly as full as the first. Jo removed the hose and pinched it shut, then stoppered the second bottle and placed it on the coffee table next to the first. She looked at the third bottle, trying to decide what she wanted more: to get warm or be done. Her teeth started chattering again, and that decided it.

She stood. A wave of dizziness assailed her. Although it had never happened to her when she'd given blood, she remembered that the technicians told people to stand up slowly because they might be dizzy. They also offered orange juice and cookies—sugar. Maybe she needed something like that. And then she remembered that for these moments while she was collecting the blood, she was dying again.

There was probably more going on here than just the loss of a pint of blood and some chills.

She shrugged off the afghan, feeling the chill more strongly, and headed carefully to the kitchen. Orange juice wasn't a staple in her refrigerator, but she had plenty of sugar—and a lukewarm cup of tea still sitting on the counter from earlier. She popped it into the microwave to heat it, stirred two spoonfuls of sugar into it, and downed it while leaning against the counter. *Too sweet, but hopefully effective.* Then, she walked back to the living room, stoked the coals in the fireplace and threw another log on the fire.

She took her place against the sofa, pulled the afghan back around her shoulders and dropped the tiny hose into the third bottle. She leaned her head back against the sofa and closed her eyes. *The sugar seems to be doing the trick,* she thought. She was no longer light-headed—just tired. *And still cold, dammit.* She pulled the afghan tighter.

Jo leaned her head back against the sofa and passed out.

CHAPTER 24

NEARLY AN HOUR LATER, POURNELLE materialized in the small hallway inside Jo's apartment, crackling blue light surrounding him. He squeezed his eyes shut as fiery pain washed over his skin and he finally slid through her wards. *Damn.* He thought that would have been easier. *She's good at what she does.*

"Jo?" He listened. Was she in the bedroom or the dining room? He didn't want to startle her—but he had to tell her about the bottles he'd left before she did something stupid. He shouldn't have disappeared so precipitously earlier. "Don't be alarmed, Jo—it's just me. Pournelle."

A log popped on the coals in the hearth and then settled.

Assuming Jo must be in the living room, he walked in that direction.

She lay propped against the sofa, her head lolled all the way back. Her hands had fallen to her sides. She was pale—more pale than Pournelle had ever seen her before. Pale enough to be—

"Christ on a crutch!" Pournelle said, racing toward her and kneeling. He tugged the needle from her hand, tossing it to the covered floor, and raised her hand above her head. He gently slapped her face. She didn't respond. Her skin was cold, but she was breathing—barely.

What to do? His healing powers were mostly cosmetic, at best, allowing him to seal a wound or alleviate the pain of some bruising.

Anything more depleted his own power and might even kill him. But he had to help her—or watch her die.

She needed blood, obviously. He was accustomed to dealing with blood, usually animal blood, though. But he could do this. He *had* to do this. He sat down beside her.

He mumbled a few words under his breath and his suit jacket disappeared, leaving him in his crisp white shirt, the sleeve already rolled to the elbow on his left arm. He pushed the afghan off Jo, mumbling more words. The necessary medical equipment appeared in their arms: one silver needle piercing the large artery in his wrist, and the other in the vein inside the bend of Jo's elbow. A flexible tube joined the two needles together.

Pournelle slumped down next to her, waiting for the transfusion apparatus to do its work, then spied the scarab necklace on the coffee table. He grabbed it and placed the chain around her neck, feeling overwhelming relief. Jo was going to be okay. She *had* to be okay.

If there was ever an up-side of being a demon, it was times like this.

Twenty minutes later he was glad for the fire as he began to grow cold. He noticed some color in Jo's cheeks, so mumbled the words that made the transfusion equipment disappear—and the small wounds on his wrist and her inner-elbow heal. Fatigue hit him then, having used too much of his magic at once. He was stranded on this plane for a few hours—and possibly here in this apartment...unless he wanted to *walk*. He made a small grimace of revulsion, shaking his head at the same time. *Uh, no.* He didn't walk if he didn't have to. Sticking around wasn't such a bad thing. He could keep an eye on Jo.

He couldn't lose her—or her friendship. It had been so very long since he'd had a true friend. And he had a good feeling about Jo in that regard.

Her eyelids fluttered open.

"Pournelle?" Her voice was thready. Weak.

"Right beside you."

She lifted her head and looked at him, then slumped back against the sofa again. "How did you get in here? The place was warded."

He rolled down his shirt sleeve and buttoned the cuff, back to his aloof self. "Why am I not surprised that that is the first thing out of your mouth? Aren't you the least bit worried about *you?*"

She shook her head, a tiny little motion that Pournelle barely caught. "Not at all. You're here." She smiled slightly, and her eyes fluttered shut again.

That brought him up short. She saw him as a hero? No. That couldn't be right. He needed to disabuse her of the notion as soon as she was capable of hearing it—no need to bombard her with it now— or the fact that she had demon blood running through her veins.

"So?" She prompted him.

"If you must know—" He cleared his throat. "I left something of mine the last time I was here. It let me slip through your barrier—quite painfully, I might add. Your wards are strong." He hadn't wanted to admit that. But he didn't want her to worry that something else might be able to make it through her wards.

"What did you leave?"

"I should tell you, so you can scour your apartment to find and dispose of it?"

"You should tell me, so I don't accidentally *dispose* of it while I'm cleaning." She moved the arm he'd placed over her head back to her lap.

"There's little likelihood of that," he said, thinking of *it*, resting on the door frame above the bathroom. Then again, maybe there was. Jo was probably the kind of person who regularly dusted door frames. He should move it. "I'll take it with me when I leave." Though he planned to do nothing of the sort. He'd move it though. It was a good thing, having it here.

"Leave it." Her voice was stronger this time, and Pournelle smiled. "Why *are* you here?"

"To stop you from doing something stupid."

"Like dying?"

"Well, there is that, of course. It's hardly worth my conceding you the point." He stretched his legs out under the coffee table and glanced at the fire, then lifted his hand and snapped. A log disappeared from the small stack near the hearth and reappeared in the fire. "Actually, I came to tell you not to try to fill more than one bottle—"

"Oh, yeah. That was stupid."

"—because they hold far more than they appear to hold. I should have told you that when I left them." And that was as close to an apology as he was willing to get. Demons did not offer apologies.

There was silence except for the crackling fire while she seemed to be thinking about that. Pournelle wondered if she were going to get mad and accuse him of nearly killing her. She'd be right. Instead, she asked, "Then why give me three?"

"Because they're handy."

When Jo laughed, Pournelle knew that all was forgiven.

CHAPTER 25

JO FELT REMARKABLY FIT THE NEXT MORNING. SHE would have thought that almost dying by pouring nearly all of her blood into magical holding vessels would have left her feeling the slightest bit hung over—even with a demon-blood transfusion. Instead, she felt fit and energetic—the best she'd felt in a while now. Was that *because* of the demon blood?

Pournelle had been reluctant to admit that he'd given her his blood, and insisted that his timely intervention—and the scarab—had won the day. But when he'd sworn he'd done nothing magical to help her feel better—that demons had very limited healing abilities—she knew there'd been something more. Only when she'd pressed had he confessed about the transfusion—and that he had no idea how it would affect her.

She didn't have time to dwell on it, but she was going to ride this energetic high as long as she could. Both she and Sheila were on borrowed time, after all. Breaking the death spells meant that the demons were going to come after her. So, she had to find a way to capture the demons—or immobilize them in some way once they'd arrived—so she could kill them. She'd never killed a living creature before, but she would do whatever it took to break the death spell, keep everyone safe and send a message to any demon vying for supremacy over them.

She finished her tea, tidied up the kitchen, and jogged down the stairs to the shop. She settled the filigree demon glasses on the bridge of her nose and laid the demon spell book on the counter in front of her. "Show me the best spell to capture or immobilize demons."

She waited. Several seconds passed, and she was about to command the book again when it finally slammed open, pages whipping over—slowly this time—until it settled open near the end of the book. It was almost as if the tome had a mind of its own, attempting *not* to fulfill the request.

To Catch a Demon was written across the top of the left-hand page in bold letters. Instructions followed. The right-hand page contained a drawing of a pentacle—not a pentagram— encased in a square box.

Pentacle. White magic—with the top-most point of the five-pointed star drawn due north, not upside-down, as in a pentagram. The drawing looked familiar, even with all the demon script written in the box's outline and in the spaces between the circle surrounding the star.

Jo pulled an old research binder from the shelf above the store window and opened it, and turned to the back section where she kept hand-drawn pictures of various things she'd come across. She found it after a few moments, a diagram quite similar to that in the demon book: a circle inside a circle inside a circle and then one more. All encased in a square. But this drawing contained a cross in the very center, the four points of which were capped with smaller crosses. No pentacle. And all the writing in the open spaces of this diagram was in Latin or Hebrew.

She'd found the picture some years ago in a translation of a Latin text, *Clavicula Salomonis*, often falsely attributed to King Solomon. The diagram was referred to as King Solomon's Key, sometimes called a demon trap. Any demon that stepped within the outermost line was trapped, held captive within the plot until the outer line was broken in some way.

Jo pulled her hand-drawn diagram from the binder and laid it side-by-side with the demon book's rendition, comparing the two.

Visually, the diagrams looked nearly identical except the demon drawing contained a pentacle in the center of the diagram, while the one from the *Clavicula* contained the cross in the very center. There had to be some difference in the text written in all the open spaces of the lines.

Jo gathered both a Latin dictionary and a Hebrew dictionary from her storeroom and returned to the counter, determined to translate the words incorporated in the *Salomonis* diagram. First, she drew a new diagram, copying everything exactly except for the pentacle and cross in the center. Then, she started translating the Latin and the Hebrew and comparing it to the demon, which she could read and understand with ease while wearing the glasses. She wrote all the translated phrases in English.

Still, it was giving her a headache, all this translation. But in a few hours' time, with her Latin and Hebrew dictionaries at her elbow, and another Hebrew dictionary open via the Internet on her phone, Jo was able to discern the difference between the two drawings: the pentacle. That was it. All the Hebrew and Latin and *Demon* writing was the same.

She had two sources—two opposing sources—claiming the diagram would bind demons to it. But which should she use? The pentacle or the cross? She was torn. She took a deep breath, leaned against the counter to rest her weary back, and removed the demon glasses, setting them into their little coffin-like box so she wouldn't accidentally break them.

The room remained brightly lit, and she could still see the tiny printed numbers on price tags across the room.

Her heart started thudding, and heaviness seemed to fill her. She sat on the stool, just looking around. It was done. For better or worse, she had the demon sight.

She looked around the room again—*really* looked around the room. Slowly, taking in the stillness of the place, early, without customers. Dust motes danced in a sunbeam. Incense smoke whorled around both. The scent of strawberries—she needed to change that for today—permeated the store. Except for the rumble of traffic on the street outside, it was quiet. Still. Peaceful.

And yet she doubted. No, *feared.*

Then, when nothing seemed to be out of the ordinary, she changed her mind again. Maybe there was little to fear in the way of evil—except when one was specifically a target of something evil—like she was now. Did she really need all the warding and protection? She saw nothing amiss. Perhaps, once this current threat was neutralized, she didn't need to be so careful. Maybe she worried too much.

Jo had thought having the demon sight would open her up to seeing evil everywhere. Maybe, instead, it would show her that evil wasn't as prevalent as she assumed. She sighed, blowing out a deep breath she hadn't realized she'd been holding. She relaxed.

And that's when she saw it. *Them.* The worms burrowing up through the wood of the shelves. Wriggling fingers, capped with eyeless, toothy maws, making their way out of the woodwork to chew through her merchandise.

A shadow slipped through the front door without a sound, pausing just inside the door. It had the vague shape of a man, but was completely dark, a faceless silhouette. It raised an arm, ran it across the flat surface of the shelf where her incense burned, and deposited a multitude of spider-like shadows, which swiftly disbursed, crawling off in all directions of the compass point.

The shadow traveled through the rest of the store, touching a shelf here, a rack there, depositing more and more of the tiny creatures. The worms continued to burrow up out of the woodwork, freeing themselves and inching along any flat surface.

Finally, the shadow man passed through the back wall of the shop without a sound, leaving his bugs behind.

A whispering filled the shop, the sound of a million tiny legs shuffling across the woodwork, or that of thousands of tiny mouths chipping away at her inventory—or at least the parts that didn't repel them.

Jo ran through the store, grabbing a few things that the creatures didn't appear to like—rosemary and mugwort, salt—especially the blessed salt she'd started selling since becoming Assumpta's friend. These she sprinkled over her personal books, on the shelves, under the front counter, keeping the things away from her most precious items. The inventory she could cleanse, or replace if necessary.

It seemed to repel them, and they scurried off in droves, some just disappearing, some fleeing for the door or window.

It looked like wards were necessary after all. But first, she had to get rid of the larger problem once and for all—the demons and their curse.

Jo cleared the rear of the shop, moving some of the larger, heavier cauldrons to the back room and rolling up the carpet that covered the hardwood beneath it. She pushed the rolled carpet aside—dust bunnies whorling in confusion—and went to the back shelf of the store for some fresh chalk. Several pieces. What she was about to draw would take more than the broken stubs she made do with for lesser spells. This was going to be heavy-duty magic, and she wanted every advantage she could get.

Patches of heavy dust and dirt had settled beneath the rug, particularly in high traffic areas. *Hmm.* She wondered if it would be a good idea to base her inventory on the dirt trails? She'd think about it later.

She snapped a quick picture with her phone, then retrieved her broom and swept the dirt from the store, banishing it out the front door to the sidewalk beyond and eventually the gutter. She had no desire for it to be tramped right back in.

A damp-mopping followed, removing as much of the grime as possible, then she followed up with a ceremonial cleansing. Filling a spray bottle with water, sea salt, and essential oils of lemon and mint, Jo sprayed the area in a clockwise motion, starting from the northernmost point of the area and all the way around to the beginning.

She gave the floor a few moments to dry, then knelt and began to draw. She started with the outermost square, drawing it as large as the carpeted area, knowing that she stood to capture the demons more easily with a bigger trap than a smaller one. The carpet would conceal it once she was done.

It took over an hour, drawing the precise lines, using some string and a tack to draw the circles near perfectly. And when she got to the center she drew a pentacle—and then the cross inside it, concluding that it couldn't hurt to use both Christian and Pagan symbolism to do the job. She wasn't converting; she just recognized the innate power the Christian symbols embodied. And she'd take advantage of anything if it meant winning the battle against the demons. She was nothing if not a pragmatist.

When she was done, she stood and stretched out the kinks in her back, dusted off her hands and rubbed her knees where the hard wood floor had pressed against them.

She looked around. While she'd been working, so intent on drawing lines and writing Latin script, the tiny, creepy-crawling creatures had returned and multiplied. Thousands of them, many-legged, antlered and grotesque, hairy and smooth—some with feelers, some without—multiple eyes and blind had surrounded the diagram up to some unseen perimeter of about eight or ten inches in some places, and twelve or twenty-four in others. She rubbed her eyes, looking at the bug perimeter, and tried to find some pattern in their formation. She could see none. And then it hit her.

The cleansing spray. She'd probably been more thorough in some areas of the floor than others, spraying close to the reach of the rug, particularly in the narrow section of the shop, and spraying further afield elsewhere. Well, maybe she could spritz them right out of the shop—and follow that up with something more powerful. She needed the spray bottle again.

She stepped toward the counter and the bugs shuffled backward, away from her. She stepped again, and they did the same. Not only was the cleansing water doing its job, she had to be wearing something that was keeping them at bay. *Excellent.* Now she wouldn't have to feel the crunching, gooey mess she was likely to make, stepping into the sea of insects and crushing them beneath her feet as she ran to the counter.

She stepped carefully out of the Solomon's Key, making certain that the heavy chalk line of the outside of the diagram remained intact. As she moved forward, the creepy-crawlies moved away from her, keeping the same cushion of distance. Still, they followed her back to the counter, as though she were the Pied Piper of Mephistophelean Bugs.

Jo grabbed the bottle of cleansing water she'd used earlier, and sprayed at the encroaching, demonic insects. The pungent scent of lemon filled the shop, warring with the rosemary in the bottle and her usual strawberry incense.

She sneezed.

When she opened her eyes, all the bugs were gone. And the room was dimmer—more like her normal, pre-demon sight vision. She glanced toward the back of the store. She couldn't read the tags on the merchandise. She gasped. *The demon sight was gone? No way.*

The sneeze. Jo clamped her eyes shut, squeezed them as tightly as she could, then opened them again to blinding light, the ability to see the tags across the room again and more Dr. Seuss bugs than she ever wanted to see in one lifetime. *Bingo. Demon vision.*

She had not expected something like that—the ability to turn the vision off and on—but she had no time to dwell on it. The bugs were encroaching. She sprayed again.

The insects hissed and writhed as the spray touched them, others fled the cone-shaped spray as if before a flamethrower. The water, where it fell and soaked into the floor, created a barrier against them. Jo sprayed all around her, pushing the bugs back farther, and then sprayed herself from her shoes up, for good measure.

Did the bugs chase her now that they knew she could see them? Or had they been here all along, and she was only now aware of them? She shivered. *Ew.* She'd hate to think that they were crawling all over her all the time. It was another question for Pournelle.

Safe in her *no bug zone*, she went back to the demon book sitting on the counter. She had created a trap. Now she needed a way to get the demons into it. And some bait.

She had an idea.

CHAPTER 26

JO PHONED ASSUMPTA. "I KNOW WHAT WE NEED to do. I need your help to set up some things in the store."

"I'll be right there," Assumpta said.

"Bring the medallion." There was a pause, and then Jo could hear Assumpta breathing heavy on the other end of the line. She was already panicking. "I thought it wasn't going to come to this," she said. "You couldn't find another way?"

"It's not what you think," Jo said. "You won't have to hand it over to demons. I'm not going to use it—" She took a deep breath, knowing she was going to toss another accusation at Assumpta, even though she had no proof, though she was fairly certain she was right... "—and *you* won't have to use it against them yourself."

Assumpta gasped. "How did you know I was considering that?"

"We've been friends long enough for me to figure out how you think. If you don't want to relinquish it, what's the next best action? I think you'd put it on again and order the demons away." Jo switched the phone to her other ear. "You'd sacrifice your soul to save your family."

That was no exaggeration. Assumpta had told her that using the medallion blackened one's immortal soul and made it impure. She'd said that impure souls head straight to Hell once freed from the body upon death. No passing go, no collecting two-hundred dollars. Each

159

use stained the soul darker...and Assumpta had told her she'd used the medallion more than once. How dark were the stains on her soul? How much more could her soul withstand before she tipped the scales permanently toward Hell?

That was never going to happen if Jo could help it.

"But—"

"No buts. Just bring it. *Please*. I'll explain everything when you get here. I told you I'd find a solution." With that enigmatic statement, she hung up. Jo touched the scarab necklace hanging around her neck, and hoped with all her might it would be enough to protect her when all was said and done.

Twenty-five minutes later, Assumpta rapped on the door of the shop. Jo let her in, locking the door behind her. It wasn't time to open yet.

Assumpta gripped the handles of her purse with two hands, her face grim, and Jo knew she carried the necklace inside. It was a powerful weapon—but only when worn. Assumpta might have had an easier time of it wearing it to the shop. Nothing could have taken the medallion from her then. Nothing could have hurt her. She would have been nearly invincible. But Jo could understand Assumpta's reluctance to don it again.

"What in God's name is that?" Assumpta asked, nodding toward the chalked diagram on the floor.

"King Solomon's Key," Jo replied, a half-smile on her face. "Come on, help me cover it up, and I'll explain everything."

"Cover it?"

"With the carpet—I can't lift it myself. We need to hide the trap from the demons, and I don't want to smear the chalk lines." Jo tried to lighten the mood. "If the demons see it, they'll run screaming in the other direction."

"Really?" Assumpta asked dryly. "Screaming? *Bull*." Her eyes were smiling, even if her lips weren't. And she still had a stranglehold on the straps of her purse.

"Okay, screaming might have been pushing it." Jo walked over to the rolled-up rug. "Come on, just help me move this thing. It's heavy."

"You managed to move the carpet last night in order to draw this monstrosity," Assumpta said, but she walked toward the rolled-up carpet, slinging the long strap of her purse over her body so she could use her hands to lift.

"I shoved it out of the way last night, but if I shove it back this morning I'll smudge the chalk lines. If we want to trap any demons, the lines need to be perfectly sound. Help me position it at the top of the diagram so we can just roll the carpet over it." Jo squatted near one end of the rolled carpet and waited for Assumpta to grab the other end. "On three, please." She bent her knees and grasped the carpet roll from the bottom. "One, two, three."

On three, they heaved the carpet up and walked around to the top of the diagram. "Don't step on the lines," Jo said, and laid the carpet just above the top of the chalked square. Assumpta lowered her end gently. Once the carpet was in place, Assumpta resumed her death-grip on the shorter handles of her purse, keeping the bag tightly closed.

Jo carefully rolled the carpet over the trap, then checked her watch. She walked to the front door and unlocked it, turning the *Closed* sign to *Open,* and motioned Assumpta over to the counter where they could both sit down and relax for a few moments.

Assumpta sat, dropping her large purse in her lap, but she didn't release her white-knuckled, *kung-fu* grip on the handles. "You look tired," she said to Jo. "How are you feeling?"

Jo nodded. "Energetic, actually." And she would tell Assumpta all about it later—the blood collection and the demon-blood transfusion. And the demon sight. "We need to act quickly. I *want* to act quickly. Now that I know what to do, I just want it done." She pulled two mugs from beneath the counter and reached for the teapot atop the samovar. "I want to feel better." She poured golden-orange tea into both mugs and pushed the sugar toward Assumpta.

"You're getting sicker—despite the scarab?"

"No—it's not that." Jo sipped her tea, letting the citrus-peach fluid warm her from the inside. "I've been doing a lot of reading from the demon book. There's so much evil in there, so much malice. I want to be done with it all. Done with them. *Fuckers.*"

Assumpta raised her eyebrows.

"Language, I know," Jo said smiling. "It's just the way I'm feeling right now. Riled up and angry. It makes me want to cuss. I want them obliterated."

"Obliterated?"

"Annihilated. Destroyed. Sent back to Hell." She looked up at Assumpta with a determined look on her face. "Whatever it takes. I want to feel clean again."

"That book is affecting you."

Jo shook her head. "Not like you think. It's not tempting me to do anything evil. It's not making me have evil thoughts. It's just that fighting fire with fire, as it were, is not as simple as I thought it would be. When all of this is said and done, I'm going to purify me and the shop top to bottom, even if I have to close up for a few days to do it. I feel dirty."

Assumpta took a sip of her own tea, put the mug back on the counter, and resumed her death-grip on her purse straps. Jo nodded at her hands. "As for the medallion, we can lock it up while we prepare."

Jo bent low behind the counter, retrieved a pad-locked, metal box and laid it on the counter. She unlocked it, and opened the lid to the left, the hinges squeaking as they rubbed together. "You're going to lock the medallion in with the evil witch's spell book?"

"Yes, and not just with the witch's spell book. I've got the demon spell book locked up in here, too." Jo tilted the metal box so Assumpta could see both books inside. "But it's only for the time being." She held out her hand for the necklace.

"But those books are evil."

"Isn't the medallion?"

Assumpta fidgeted on the stool. "Yeah, but...it can be used for good, too. And it helped me to see the true form of the demons I was dealing with."

"Both of these books can be used for good." *Intent, intent, intent,* she thought to herself. She and Assumpta were having this conversation a lot lately, it seemed. "Are you certain that using the medallion was an act of goodness?"

"It allowed me to break free of my demon mark—"

"It helped you get rid of your mark by allowing you to command a demon. *Command a demon!* What kind of *good* people command demons?" Jo gave her a pointed look, feeling a twinge of remorse at her strong words.

"But the outcome was good." Still keeping one hand firmly wrapped around her purse, Assumpta grasped the mug of hot tea and lifted it to her lips, blowing across the top of it softly before sipping.

Jo let out a heavy sigh. What could she say to that? "You're absolutely right." She pushed the metal box toward Assumpta. "And we should lock it up while we're making our preparations."

Indecision clouded Assumpta's face, but she opened her purse and pulled out a bulky, plastic-wrapped package, surrounded by a rosary. Instead of placing it into the box, she handed the necklace to Jo.

The plastic felt cold in Jo's hand. If she remembered correctly, Assumpta had dropped the necklace into a plastic bag containing a mixture of holy water and holy salt, bagged it inside another plastic bag, and then wrapped the entire package in a blessed rosary in order to keep demons away from it. She gave it a little squeeze. Squishy. "The books and medallion might actually do well together in the box, with the necklace protecting the books, should anybody—or any*thing*—come looking for it."

"And it might be cause for celebration if someone took your box," Assumpta said, wary look on her face. "They'll be getting three for one, as it were."

Jo grinned. "I don't think we have anything to worry about. I told you, I have a plan."

CHAPTER 27

A SSUMPTA LOOKED AT JO WITH RAISED eyebrows. "So, what's the plan?"

"It's simple." Jo placed the medallion into the metal box next to the witch's spell book, and retrieved the demon spell book. She opened the cover, turning the tissue-thin pages gently until she reached a marked section. "Here's the spell that is going to fix everything—" She tapped her finger on the top of the page. "—well, almost everything. We'll still have to break the death spell. But after that, we're home free."

"What does the spell do?"

"It banishes demons back to Hell."

Assumpta looked at the page, then turned her head away quickly, eyes blinking rapidly. "So, you don't intend to kill the demons?"

"Only if I must. Right now, I plan to send them back to where they belong. By the time they get here, the death spell will be broken. We'll lure them onto the rug, trapping them in the Solomon's Key. They won't be able to escape, and they won't be able to use their powers against us. It should be relatively easy to banish them—a simple matter of working the spell."

"Do you want me to invite Father Tony? Pournelle?"

"That's not part of my plan."

"Then, you'd better lay it out for me. I'm not sure what you intend to do with the medallion—or what I'm supposed to do while you work the spells. Do you think it's wise for just the two of us to handle this?"

"The plan is simple: First I work the counter-spell to free Sheila and me. Then, we work a spell to lure the demons here, using the medallion. We trap them, and then we send them back to Hell. Once the demons are back in Hell, they can't harm us anymore."

"But what about the next time?"

Jo closed the demon book and pushed it aside. "There won't be a next time—not with these demons."

Assumpta did not look convinced. "How can you be certain?"

"Because according to the spell, forcing them back to Hell weakens them and strips them of the majority of power they've gained. Pournelle said as much earlier; the book confirms it. It will take the demons decades, probably longer, to build up that much strength again. We'll be safe."

"And what about different demons?"

"We'll cross that bridge when we come to it."

Assumpta was nodding, taking in everything Jo was saying. "Ok—but why do you need the medallion?"

Jo took a deep breath, knowing Assumpta wasn't going to like the answer. But there was no way around it. "It's the bait to lure the demons here. I need something to draw them to us before they realize the death spell is broken."

"Bait! You can't leave the medallion unprotected. What happens if things go wrong and the demons take it? There will be no stopping them."

"Hear me out." Jo walked around the counter and to the far side of the carpet they'd just moved. "We place the medallion here on a small table—on the far side of Solomon Key—where the demons can see the medallion from the door—but will be forced to walk across the Key in order to get to it. I've drawn the Key nearly as large as the carpet, so once they've stepped onto it, we know they're trapped. They won't even be able to reach the table—"

"But how are we going to let them know the medallion is up for grabs?"

"With a *lure* spell from the book—the medallion will be its focus. That's how we'll let our aggressors know that we have the medallion in the store. They'll come running."

"Which puts the medallion in jeopardy. It could be stolen by *anyone* while it's just sitting there on the table." Assumpta seemed angry. Was she miffed at Jo, or just situation? "How could you even consider using it as bait—knowing I need to get it back to Saint Michael?"

Jo smiled. "That's why this plan is so perfect—and it's where your help comes in," she said. You'll need to call on Saint Michael and let him know that you're ready to return the medallion. He simply needs to be here in the shop at the appointed time. Since he'll be here—he'll protect us all from the demons should things get out of hand. By the time everything is over, the death spell will be broken. We'll banish the demons who wrought it. And you'll get to turn over a dangerous artifact to Saint Michael—thereby erasing whatever type of sin that's been clouding up your soul. Win-win-win." Jo was practically bouncing with excitement. She hadn't had this much energy in a long time. She felt really good about this, and nearly skipped back to the counter.

"What about Father Tony?"

"I don't think we need him here." Jo took a pair of scissors and snipped a two-inch sprig of rosemary from a new plant sitting on the counter. While they talked, she pulled the rosemary leaves from the stem and put them in a pile on a sheet of waxed paper.

"But I do." Assumpta hooked a foot around the leg of the stool and leaned her elbows on the counter. "He can provide protections that you can't—"

"But—"

"And he can pray, gather us some divine help in addition to Saint Michael—should Saint Michael decide to aid us." The last was said with more hope than conviction. "It will make me feel better if he's here."

"Okay, then" Jo said, convinced that, if nothing else, Assumpta would be reassured enough by the presence of the priest, that things would run more smoothly. "If it will make you feel better, you can invite him. He can always ramp up the exorcism if he thinks we need it."

Or if the trap fails. She didn't expect that to happen, but Assumpta was right. It couldn't hurt to use all the back-up they had access to.

Jo placed the demon book back in the metal box, locked it, and shoved it under the counter.

"What else do we need to do to put this plan into action?" Assumpta clipped a sprig of rosemary and added its leaves to the wax paper.

Jo smiled. "I'm glad you asked. I'll be standing on the other side of the Solomon's Key, out of most of harm's way, but I think we'll need you behind the counter. It would be suspicious if we were all standing around the medallion. So—we'll need a circle of protection for you."

Jo lifted the foam mat she kept on the hardwood behind the front glass counter and leaned it against the wall. Standing all day was a bitch without some kind of cushion.

"Chalk?" At Jo's nod, Assumpta grabbed a fresh piece from the box on the counter and handed it to Jo. Jo traced a circle on the polished wooden boards, as large as she could make it between the front wall of the store and the counter. She drew the line wide and thick, but left room for additional circles beyond it. Assumpta moved Jo's stool and pushed a few boxes into the nearby store room to make additional room. "I'm not taking any chances with this circle—or with you," Jo said. "It has to be strong."

"Triple protection?" Assumpta pulled out her holy water and blessed salt and set them on the floor at Jo's elbow.

"Yes, and more." Jo finished the chalk circle and stood. She retrieved a bottle of rosemary essential oil and handed it to Assumpta, then cut several more sprigs from the rosemary bush on the counter and added them to the pile she'd started earlier. "Rosemary for additional protection—oil *and* crushed rosemary sprigs."

Assumpta nodded. "I love the way this stuff smells." She uncorked the essential oil and wet her thumb, then knelt and began drawing a wide, oily circle outside the chalk one. "You know, Father Tony could help with cleansing and protecting, too."

Jo wondered why she felt so reluctant to accept more than Father Tony's just-in-case help. Could it be she just wasn't up for another of his lectures? Maybe it *would* be better to have his prepared help instead of *reactionary* help in the case that something went wrong.

Jo sighed. *In for a penny, in for a pound*, she thought. "If it will make you feel better, tell Father Tony to prepare for a demonic war. And while you're at it, you might want to start sending out feelers to Saint Michael."

"About that—"

"Yeah, I know—" Jo gave her a sympathetic smile. "He hasn't been in contact since you refused to give him the demon necklace. But here's his chance to get it back. I'm certain he'll come to get it."

"But what if he doesn't?"

"He'll come if you ask. I know it."

Assumpta stopped making the rosemary-oil circle and looked up at Jo. "How can you have such faith?"

Jo smiled. "Because the alternative is unthinkable." She got down on her hands and knees and laid slivers of rosemary along the oiled line. "I'll take over here if you want to make your calls. Use the storeroom if you want."

Assumpta stood and dusted off her knees. "When do you want to do this?"

"Things here are nearly in place." There was just one little ingredient she needed to get the ball rolling... She sat back on her heels and gave Assumpta a thoughtful glance. "It wouldn't do to trouble Father Tony more than once to come down here. Why don't you find out when he's got an hour or two free and we'll do it then? But it's got to be soon—tonight, or perhaps early tomorrow."

"Caroline's funeral is tomorrow."

Jo froze. She'd been so engrossed with all the preparations, she hadn't given that any thought. She hadn't even asked Assumpta how she was handling it. "I'm sorry."

Assumpta nodded. "It's okay. I'm working through it." She stepped toward the storeroom. "Just give me a minute or two."

Well, that could have gone better, Jo thought, when the door shut behind Assumpta. She laid more rosemary in the oil, continuing to reinforce the circle behind the counter, putting all the positive energy into it that she could muster. She thickened the chalk line, added more rosemary oil, holy water and salt, and wished she had some of Father Tony's chrism—but that stuff was hard to come by. Father Tony wouldn't give any up, and she wasn't going to steal from a priest. Maybe Assumpta could get him to bend his convictions.

A few moments later, Assumpta stepped out of the storeroom and scooped up her purse.

Jo sat back on her heels. "That was quick. All done?"

"I sent up a brief message to Saint Michael, but I don't know if he's listening." She grimaced. "Father Tony wants to talk to me in person."

"Uh-oh."

"Yeah," Assumpta grimaced. "I'm probably in for confession and penance this afternoon. But the fact that Father Tony wants to see me is encouraging. If he wasn't willing to do this, he probably would have just yelled at me over the phone."

"Ah. Was he very disappointed in you?" Jo repressed a smile.

"Very," Assumpta agreed. "And he wants to hear the entire story—*at leisure*—in his office."

Jo dusted her hands and stood. "Then you'd better be going."

"Yeah. I'll call you in a couple hours." Assumpta left, causing the fairies and dragons hanging from the ceiling to dance in the slight breeze of the opening door.

CHAPTER 28

ASSUMPTA CALLED TWO HOURS AND FIFTEEN minutes later. "Six o'clock tonight?"

"Perfect." Jo said, pushing aside rosemary clippings and chalk to clear some counter space. "Things went okay?"

"Yes—I kept explanations short and sweet. Father Tony will be happy to help out."

Jo couldn't imagine Father Tony being happy about what was going on. "How about confession?"

"Avoided for the moment, but I have a feeling I'll be on my knees tomorrow morning." There was laughter in Assumpta's voice.

Jo chuckled. "Or maybe this evening's events will convince him that confession is unnecessary."

"Highly unlikely. Is there anything I can do for you in the meantime?"

"Come early and help me dress some candles. We'll strengthen the circles, too, if I don't find time for that this afternoon."

"I should be able to get there around three," Assumpta said. "See you then."

Jo set the phone down and looked at the clock. It was early yet, —before noon. She'd had a few customers right after the shop opened, and then nothing—but that was typical. Lunchtime would bring in a steady stream.

Making a snap decision, she got some paper from the storeroom and made a sign in bold block letters: *Closed Wednesday Afternoon for Inventory*. It would be better for all concerned if she could focus on spellwork, instead of her retail duties, until tonight. She posted the sign on the door, locked up, and then returned to the counter.

She had several things that needed doing before Assumpta, Father Tony, and Saint Michael arrived tonight. She needed to break the death spell, cast the lure spell, and gather the components necessary for the banishment spell—so they'd be ready when she needed them tonight. With the store closed, there should be plenty of time.

Opening the demon book to a marked location, she reviewed the spell she would use to lure the demons to her shop. It provided a method to draw only specific demons to her by using the spoken part, which she needed to compose herself. It was tricky. Say the wrong words and she'd be calling the wrong demons. Precision was paramount—and if she got it wrong? Who knew how many demons she and Assumpta would be battling?

But what choice did she have?

Well, the alternative to the spell, was to ask Pournelle to deliver the message. But she didn't want to involve him. Sure, she could ask him to alert the demons. But did he have that kind of power? That influence? Would he be able to pinpoint the *exact* demons they needed to get the message to? So far, he hadn't been able to identify them.

Worse, asking Pournelle to use any of his connections required letting him in on the secret: that Assumpta had the demon medallion in her possession—that she had had it for a while now. Telling Pournelle at this point would only cause trouble. *Not that his knowing would affect me*, she thought.

The risk, of course, was to Assumpta. If Pournelle discovered that Assumpta had the medallion, he wouldn't be happy. What demon would—learning that he'd been in the presence of an artifact that could easily destroy him? Pournelle might even feel betrayed. He'd wonder if Assumpta had ever used it against him.

Hells! He might even think *she'd* used it against him. If Pournelle got angry, he might stop all his *good will.* And as much as she and Assumpta waffled over trusting Pournelle and using his help, they relied on it. Perhaps too much.

No, there was no choice at all. She had to use the spell.

So—how to phrase this? She wanted to let some demons know— local demons only, since they were the ones who plagued her—that the medallion would be unguarded at a certain time. It wouldn't do for demons far and wide to make their way into the city in hopes of gaining this powerful artifact. And she needed to pinpoint the very demons who both desired the medallion *and* who cast the death spell on her and Sheila. It was a very small subset, no more than three—if her dream had been correct. But probably it was only two, since the demon who'd attacked her a few days ago insisted he was merely a messenger.

She wrote out a few sample phrases on a scrap piece of paper: want a spell to send a message, to contact local demons only, to contact local demons who *menace* her, *anonymously* deliver a message to... She had to get the phrasing right in order to find the right demons.

Jo scribbled a complete sentence, changed two words, then put the pen down. She tried it aloud. "By this spell, I intend to contact the Baltimore demons who both desire the medallion and who have threatened Assumpta Mary-Margaret O'Connor's family and friends, and most specifically who have cast the death spell on me and Sheila O'Connor, now Sheila Reagan. Anonymously inform these demons, and *only* these demons, that the medallion they seek will be in The Turning Wheel in Baltimore City on display tonight at seven p.m."

Jo read it again, made two changes, and then read it a third time. Finally satisfied, she copied it out completely, mistake free, and set it aside by the glass cauldron in which she would cast the spell.

Then, she pulled all the ingredients she needed from her shelves and lined them up on the counter in three groups: one for breaking the death spell on her and Sheila, one for luring the demons to her shop, and one for banishing the demons back to Hell.

It was time to begin.

"Show me the death counter-spell," she said to the demon spell book. It slammed open, startling her in the silence of the shop. The pages turned, whipped by some unfelt wind, and finally rested open at the counter-spell.

Jo pulled the brass pot and steel knife closer to her, along with the other ingredients: purified water, rosemary, halite—which was nothing more than ordinary rock salt, but perhaps the demons didn't know that. And of course, the dead man's blood. *Her* blood.

She chopped the rosemary with the steel knife and tossed it into the pot, covering it with purified water. She added the rock salt, and as the spell demanded, briskly stirred the concoction three times *widdershins*—counter clockwise—with the knife.

As she worked, her eyes got gritty, and she found herself constantly rubbing them. Her mouth grew dry. She couldn't decide if the symptoms were because she was breaking the death spell, or because she was performing demon magic. Either way, it was uncomfortable.

While the liquid still spun in the copper pot, she poured a thin, steady stream of her blood into the swirling water, and said the words to counter the spell. Once done, she gripped the pot in both hands, and held on until the water stilled.

That was it. It was done. The spell broken.

She let out a deep sigh and released the pot, still feeling slightly nauseated. She'd expected to feel more at the spell's conclusion—receive some physical indication that that whatever magical bond existed between her and the demons had been broken. But maybe it was good that she had not. If *she* hadn't felt the spell break, then neither had the demons. So, she still had time to get everything else into place.

Jo poured a cup of tea from her magical teapot, and laced it liberally with honey. She drank it quickly, hoping to quell the nausea and bolster her energy before she worked the lure spell. While she waited for the caffeine to kick in, she cleared the space of the previous spell, setting things aside until she could ritually dispose of the used ingredients later. Then, she began the next spell.

She lit a tall, white candle and stood it upright in the center of a small, glass cauldron, then added the other spell components from several different angles in order to surround the base of the candle. She meditated on the flame for a few moments, then lifted the paper she'd written the spell on and read it aloud.

As she read, a pain worked its way up from her belly and to her throat. Her voice grew hoarse, and she felt like retching. She swallowed hard, tamping the feeling down, and finished reciting the spell. Once done, she loosely folded the paper and held it in the candle's flame, allowing it to catch fire. She held it as long as she could, until the flames licked too close to her fingers, then dropped it into the cauldron to finish burning. She watched it burn, hands at her lips, while her stomach continued to roil. When there was nothing left but ashes, the spell was complete.

She blew out the candle, then ran to the bathroom and vomited. And even though she emptied the meager contents of her stomach, the pain persisted. With shaking legs, she returned to the counter, freshened her tea, and sat. She was certain now, that her physical ailments were a byproduct of working the demon magic. There could be no other explanation. She hoped they wouldn't get any worse. She had at least one more demon spell to work tonight.

But now she'd arrived at the moment she'd been dreading. She turned to the banishment spell. In order to work it, she needed demon blood.

Demon blood! And there was only one way she knew how to get some.

She opened the cash register drawer and pulled out Pournelle's white calling card and read from it, the letters burning up as she spoke. "Pournelle Ahb—"

Before she uttered the last syllable of his name, he appeared. He wore a tailored, black tuxedo, and held a glass of what she assumed was champagne in one hand. Tiny bubbles rose up through the amber liquid and popped on the surface. He gave her a disapproving look. "Always catching me at the most inopportune times..." he muttered.

Jo stared at him. "Is that glitter on your shoulders?"

He brushed it off with a practiced hand, his face the epitome of ennui. "I was at a *party*. What can I do for you?"

"At one in the afternoon?"

"It's *not* afternoon where I'm partying."

I'm partying—her mind repeated his phrase. She raised her eyebrows. *Pournelle partied?* It was such a curious thought she didn't think to temper her request. "I need some demon blood."

He stalked to the counter and set the champagne flute down on the glass top with a clink. He leaned in close to Jo, almost growling the words, and she could smell the sulfur on him. "You need demon blood?"

Was he angry? Jo leaned away from him. *Why* was he angry? She nodded, silent.

"Just what spell are you planning to work, Ms. Byrne?"

Yes, he was very angry. Jo hadn't realized he'd known her last name, let alone would invoke it when he was upset. But what was he upset about? She pushed the book toward him, tapping a finger on the page, knowing he couldn't read which spell it was. But she wouldn't actually tell him. It might piss him off more. "This one."

"You know I can't read from that book," he said through grinding teeth. "Which spell?"

"It's better you don't know," Jo said.

He slapped his hand down on the counter. "You want me to give you *my* blood, and you won't tell me which spell you're going to cast?"

"It's not your blood I wanted!" Jo was mortified. She hadn't even considered asking Pournelle for his own blood. "I just thought it might be easy for you to get some for me. It didn't even cross my mind to have you open a vein."

He seemed to calm.

Jo ventured, "But if you were willing..." She shrugged. "Wouldn't that be the easiest thing?"

"Willing?" Pournelle seemed to bite the word off, it was so clipped. *Nope. Not calm yet.* "I only need a few drops for this spell."

He picked up the champagne flute. "You have no idea what you're asking."

"It's only a few drops." She shrugged. "A needle prick. Less than a paper cut—I apologize if this is a terrible imposition. It's important."

He glared at her. Drained the flute and transferred it to his left hand, then raised his right and snapped. He was gone.

Jo exhaled, her heart thumping. *So much for that*, she thought. Was there a way around the demon blood? And would the demon book tell her? She turned to the tome and closed it. "Can I substitute anything for a demon's blood in the banishment spell and obtain the same results?"

The book shot open in its usual fashion, pages turning as if caught in their own personal whirlwind. The pages stopped, about halfway open, on two blank pages. As she watched, writing appeared, written letter-by-letter by an invisible hand: *The blood of humans leading corrupt and evil lives may be substituted for demon blood, for in the end they will be demons. The closer the corrupt human is to death, the more potent the blood will be. Twice the amount of blood will be required in substitution.*

"Great," muttered Jo. "So, all I need to do is take a cab to the North Branch Correctional Facility and ask a serial killer to donate a few drops of blood. Pournelle probably wouldn't have a problem with that." She slammed the book shut, wishing she'd thought to ask about substitutions in the first place.

"I wouldn't have a problem with what?" Pournelle asked, appearing on the other side of the counter.

Jo gasped, her heart racing. "We really need to get you a bell. You couldn't have phoned first?"

He shrugged. Gone was the glitter on his tux and the champagne flute. He laid a small, brown bottle on the counter in front of Jo. "Here's the blood you need."

Cautiously, Jo picked up the bottle. It was glass, the screw-on cap metal, and similar to the old-fashioned mecuricome bottle she'd once seen in the medicine cabinet in her grandmother's house. She lifted it to the light and tilted it, watching the thick fluid move from side to side. The bottle held an ounce, if that. But it was plenty more than she needed.

"Thank you," Jo said, sitting the bottle down again. "I really didn't expect more than few—"

"It's not mine," Pournelle said, anger still clipping his words. "Don't ask me for something like this again."

He raised his hand and snapped, disappearing, and one of his white calling cards fluttered down to the surface of the counter. With a shaking hand, Jo retrieved it and tucked it into the cash register's drawer.

CHAPTER 29

JUST BEFORE THREE, ASSUMPTA KNOCKED ON THE door of the shop and Jo let her in, leaving the door unlocked. Assumpta wore jeans and a polo shirt, her long hair pulled back in a ponytail. She crossed to the front counter and set the large paper bag she carried on top of it. "Father Tony should arrive at four."

"Excellent," Jo said, though she didn't feel the same confidence Assumpta did in the middle-aged priest; she wished he didn't have to be here. But if his presence made Assumpta more comfortable, so be it.

She snuffed the strawberry incense she incessantly burned and lit eucalyptus instead. Eucalyptus—to purify the shop of strawberry and other odors. Eucalyptus for its fresh scent and for new beginnings. Eucalyptus to cleanse her mind.

A thin tendril of smoke drifted up to her nose. She inhaled deeply, breathing in the crisp aroma and picturing a steady wind breezing through her store—and her mind—chasing out impurities and leaving freshness behind. She blew out a deep breath, forcing the scoria from her lungs, pushing them out of her body—it wasn't exactly a spell or a ritual. It just seemed like the right thing to do at the moment—and it seemed to be helping her nausea. "I'm almost ready," she said to Assumpta, giving her an assessing look. "Are you certain you want to be here? You can still change your mind, you know. And,

179

you won't hurt my feelings if you decide to bail. I'm certain I can work with Father Tony and avoid us coming to blows." *As much as I'd rather not work with Father Tony,* she thought, smiling and only half joking.

Assumpta shook her head. "No—this is all my fault. I've got to be here and see things through."

Jo gave her an exasperated look. "We've been over this already." She blew on the cone of eucalyptus, making the tip glow bright red. When she stopped blowing, a long, thick swirl of smoke eddied up. She placed the cone in the brass dish on the high shelf by the door and walked toward Assumpta. "What's going to happen tonight was meant to be. Imagine that you and I were not friends—" She paused and raised an eyebrow, looking Assumpta straight in the face. They both burst out laughing. "Yeah, I find that hilarious, too. But still, assume we weren't friends—we'd *still* be in this situation. We'd be having a similar conversation—"

"But—"

"Hear me out." When Assumpta nodded, Jo continued. "At some point you would have figured out on your own that demons had cursed your friends and family. They would have attacked you personally, or someone else, and given you the same ultimatum. You would have considered the alternatives, including giving over the medallion, but you would have tried other avenues first. Father Tony, while well-meaning—and your apparent direct conduit to God—is ineffective in anything more than a supporting role. And you know that. You might even have left him out of the loop completely, if not for your past. I grant that he's well intentioned, but he doesn't see the larger picture through his Catholic blinders. That could get you into trouble."

"He's not that bad." Assumpta stepped behind the counter—into the circles of protection—and started emptying her paper bag, setting holy water, blessed salt and four tall pillar candles on the counter beside a sheet of waxed paper covered in rosemary leaves. "And he helped Greg with his exorcism." She folded the paper bag and tucking it under the counter.

Jo picked up the candle closest to her, wrapped in red tissue with a picture of Saint Michael on it, and tore away the paper. The wax was etched with his likeness and his name. All the candles were wrapped in colored paper, each depicting one of four of the seven archangels—Michael, Gabriel, Rafael, and Uriel. She didn't sell them in the shop, but maybe she should consider it. She said, "Okay—Father Tony isn't *that* bad—and he does have the strength of his convictions behind him, which is a usually good thing. But he's a little naive when it comes to dealing with demons and other things that go bump in the night, mainly because he's had no experience. So...you would have considered your alternatives, and maybe called on Saint Michael—who's still in the wind right now?" She looked to Assumpta for confirmation.

"Yeah, as far as I know. But I have to have faith he'll show up here tonight." She uncapped the rosemary oil Jo had left on the counter and poured some into a shallow dish beside the waxed paper.

"He will," Jo said, reaching for the Uriel candle and pushing Saint Michael's toward Assumpta. She removed the colorful paper, dipped her thumbs into rosemary oil, then coated the entire candle, pushing her thumbs firmly against the wax. Closing her eyes, she pictured a shield, protection for Assumpta, when the candle burned. Still picturing the protective shield, she rolled the candle in the rosemary leaves, getting as many to stick to the oiled wax as she could, then set it aside.

They worked in silence for a few moments, until all the candles were dressed. Then Assumpta spritzed them with holy water. "You know, we could abort the plan completely. It's not too late," Assumpta said, stowing her purse behind the counter and surveying the store. "We can find another way to save you and Sheila."

"Too late," Jo said, and Assumpta gave her a stricken look. Jo pointed to the brass pot and the glass cauldron she'd used earlier. "Sheila and I are safe. The spell is broken. I cast the counter-spell and the lure spell this afternoon. Everything is already in motion."

But Jo understood how Assumpta felt. She'd had her own misgivings—especially once she started seeing things with the demon's vision. But she had to do this. She had to get rid of the demons who'd spelled her—her, *and* Assumpta's family. Pournelle could only protect so many of them. And even if he had an unlimited supply scarabs, the demons would just find another way to do them harm. "Are you getting cold feet, Assumpta?"

"I'm worried—is that cold feet? I don't want anyone getting hurt."

"It's not like we're going to Hell..." Jo let her voice trail off, giving Assumpta an impish grin, trying to bolster her spirits.

Assumpta smiled back. "Yeah, I guess it's hard to top that one—"

"I would have never thought that possible if I hadn't seen you do it," Jo said. "It ought to be child's play to take out demons on our own turf."

"It's just that if the medallion is taken by the demons instead of Saint Michael, we'll both be in worse shape."

"Saint Michael won't let that happen. I know it." And if she thought reassuring Assumpta about Saint Michael was slightly ironic, she had no time to dwell on it.

The bell over the door tinkled and Father Tony walked in, carrying his brown, leather exorcism satchel, and his vestments in a garment bag, hanging over the other arm. The zipper pull was a Celtic Cross and dangled upside down, knocking against the hanger and making a wooden clank at each step. Father Tony set the satchel on the counter. "Good afternoon, ladies." He gave a slight bow. "I understand you have need of my services today."

Jo nodded. "Nice to see you, Father. Thanks for coming on such short notice." She eyed the garment bag. "Dressing up for us today?"

The priest smiled, laying the bag over one of the stools near the counter. "Assumpta implied that I might want to don my *spiritual armor* for today's blessings, so I brought my physical armor with me as well." He unzipped the garment bag and pulled his robes from inside. "I told her that in the case of priestly vestments, the clothes definitely *don't* make the man—but they often make the man's *attitude*. I always feel they lend my prayers more *oomph* when I'm wearing them, though I'm certain that's *not* the case."

Father Tony chuckled and thumbed the latch on his satchel and pulled it open. He eyed the dressed candles on the counter, and Jo had to give him credit for not making faces. He had to recognize the stamped-wax candles beneath the rosemary dressing—and deplore the dressing, which the Catholic Church did not condone. She should applaud him for his forbearance. Or, maybe—a doubtful maybe—he was coming around to see things her way.

"But your vestments are blessed," Assumpta said, with a curiously desperate gleam in her eye. "That offers you more protection than just your collar and jacket." And then Jo knew where Assumpta was headed with this. She hoped to provide more protection for Father Tony through his vestments. Assumpta just might be on to something there. Jo frowned, her heart sinking, as she realized Assumpta's worries ran deeper than she'd thought.

"But we have nothing to worry about here," Father Tony said.

And that was what worried Jo about Father Tony. As many times as he'd been exposed to evil, he didn't seem to realize how big a threat it was. He had his faith—which had been strengthened by his exposure in the past—and was armed with his holy water and religious zeal, but he didn't seem to *get* how much danger they were in.

"Are you ready to begin?" Jo asked Father Tony.

"No time like the present. But first I need to clean my hands and don my robes." He pulled a bottle of hand sanitizer from his satchel, rubbed some over his hands, and prayed quietly. "Give virtue into my hands, O Lord, that being cleansed from all stain I might serve You with purity of my mind and my body."

Jo bent beneath the counter and pulled out her metal box, fetching the key from the cash register and opening the padlock. She watched Father Tony out of the corner of her eye. She'd never seen the process of a priest putting on his robes, and it fascinated her—there were so many pieces.

He pulled a white square cloth from his bag, kissed it, and—while mumbling another quiet prayer—wrapped it around his shoulders, crossed it in front of his throat and tied it. Next, he pulled the long white robe from its hanger and dropped it over his head with another prayer. Still praying, he belted the robe at his waist with a braided white cord, the shiny tassels at the ends almost touching the tops of his leather shoes. He turned back to his satchel and removed his stole. She'd seen Father Tony use it before. The long purple scarf was made of a silky material and folded neatly into a square. He kissed it, and hung it around his neck, praying—again—while the ends fluttered nearly to the floor, as long as the tassels on the belt. Finally, he took out a long, poncho-like garment, heavily embroidered in green floss with a cross in the center, and beautiful leaves and ivy surrounding it.

It really reminded Jo of armor—a breastplate. Too bad it wasn't made of metal.

Father Tony lifted the pectoral cross that he always wore from underneath the robe and let it lay on top of his vestments. "Should we start from the back, as usual?"

As usual? Jo frowned. "Warding the shop is not part of the process today, Father," she said. "Today we're inviting evil *in*."

"*What?*" Father Tony looked surprised.

Jo looked to Assumpta for an explanation. That's why Father Tony seemed so casual about what was going to happen. Assumpta hadn't told him what was going on.

Assumpta shrugged. "The truth wasn't going to get him here."

Father Tony butted into the conversation. "There's a special place in Hell for people who lie to priests."

Jo chuckled. "Somehow I doubt that."

"I'm certain there's at least penance involved," Assumpta said glumly.

"At the very *least*," Father Tony agreed.

Jo chuckled and swung open the lid of the metal box.

Father Tony looked on expectantly. "Is someone going to fill me in on what's going on here today, and what you expect me to do?"

"Momentarily," Jo said, removing the demon necklace from the box. She began unwrapping it, starting with the two rosaries Assumpta had wound around the package in the shape of a cross. She dropped the rosaries to the counter-top, then unzipped the outer plastic bag and pulled out the second bag—filled with holy water and salt. Submerged within was a third plastic bag, encapsulating the necklace itself—keeping it dry from the holy water and protecting it from the corrosive salt. Assumpta had taken these precautions in order to cloak the evil from anything searching for it and to prevent anything evil from touching it, but she hadn't wanted to destroy it. Assumpta hadn't known if destroying it was even possible.

Jo could feel Father Tony's eyes on her, certainly curious about the rosaries. He must have suspected the water was holy water.

"What is that?" he asked.

"Bait," Jo said, carefully pulling the wrapped necklace from its watery prison. The medallion was made of multi-colored sea glass—soft turquoise, clear blue, and opaque white—slotted into a round bronze casement about the size of her fist. It was pretty, if old fashioned looking, and appeared innocent of evil. And it was threaded on a thick brass chain, to be worn as a necklace. Late afternoon sunshine glinted off the medallion, casting a rainbow on the ceiling.

"Bait for what?" Father Tony prompted.

"Demons," Assumpta said. "It's a lure to bring demons here to the store."

Jo clutched the medallion in her fist, feeling the smooth stones against her fingertips, and the chain hanging down on either side of her hand. It felt heavier than it looked. It was the first time she'd touched it, and she wondered if the demon presence would make itself known.

"Holy Mother of God!" Father Tony crossed himself. "Why do you want to lure demons here? Why would the demons want a necklace?" He leaned toward the necklace to get a better look at it and his pectoral cross struck the glass counter with a *thwack!* startling them all. He pressed it against his chest, stepping closer, and the confusion on his face cleared. "Wait—it's not just a necklace, is it? It's corrupt. It has some kind of power—*evil* power. What can it do?" He held up a hand. "No, don't tell me. *How* did you come by it?"

Jo opened her fingers and stared at the medallion. How much should she reveal to Father Tony? Nothing she said would win him over. But she suspected glossing over too many details would anger him. She looked to Assumpta.

Assumpta shrugged.

Father Tony turned to Assumpta. He nearly shouted, "And what do *you* know about it?"

In a small voice, Assumpta answered. "More than anyone, I suppose." Father Tony gasped. "I got it from Caroline, who got it from her fiancé. She had no idea that Adrian was a demon. She gave it to me."

"And you know what it does? What it can do?"

The fact that Adrian was a demon seemed to fly right over Father Tony's head, Jo thought—unless Assumpta had filled him in on all that? If not, she was going to have to explain an awful lot later. She didn't envy Assumpta that. She'd be doing penance for more than just lying to Father Tony.

Assumpta nodded. "Whoever wears the necklace can control demons, can compel them to do practically anything."

He stepped back from her. "Saints preserve us! You know what it does because you've used it, haven't you?"

She nodded again. "Yes. It's how I got rid of my demon mark."

"Sweet Jesus." He pulled a small, leather-bound book from his satchel and started turning pages. "We need protection. I need to reinforce all the blessings I've put upon this store." He looked at Assumpta. "And you need cleansing, prayer—"

"You can't," Jo said. "I've already dropped the wards. We need them down in order to get the demons *into* the store. I can't believe Assumpta hasn't explained everything to you."

Shamefaced, Assumpta cleared her throat and looked at Jo. "I told him you needed him to bless the store again—which you *will* need, once everything else is done."

Father Tony looked heavenward for a moment, probably praying for patience. "Please explain what's going on—and what you expect of me."

Assumpta cleared her throat. "Caroline's fiancé—Adrian—was a major demon in charge of all the demons in this area. We thought killing him would send the demons in a panic—disorganize them and send them running. But his place was quickly filled by another demon on this plane. Demetrios. And now that Demetrios is gone, others have moved in to take his place. They've threatened me, my family and my friends."

"Child, how did you come to learn so much about demon politics?" His eyes were sad, but he stood taller, the vestments actually making the man, Jo thought. He looked righteous enough to snatch a demon with his fist and squeeze the life out of it.

Jo moved around the counter to stand beside Assumpta. "When you're the target of such machinations, you learn quickly what's at stake in order to save yourself."

Father Tony set his prayer book on the counter and clasped his hands together. "She had no need to save herself! She only needed to pray. God would help her."

"God helps those who help themselves," Jo said. "Assumpta was doing what she could to help Him help her."

"Blasphemy!"

"Really?" Assumpta asked. "Think about it—at one point did praying help my demon mark? When did He step in and—"

"Silence!" Father Tony's eyes blazed. Gone was the sadness when he looked at Assumpta. "Hypocrites often use that phrase to justify their behavior. It's blasphemy when it's trotted out to defend actions not condoned by the Church."

"You can't have it both ways, Father," Assumpta said, crossing her arms on her chest. Her face was mutinous. It was amazing how the priest could turn Assumpta into a recalcitrant teen, Jo thought. But she got that.

Father Tony straightened and stood up taller. "How dare—"

"Enough!" Jo said. The two of them were never going to see eye to eye about the situation, but maybe she could get them to join sides to combat the evil. Theological discussions could wait for another day. "Father, Assumpta neglected to tell you a key issue here. We're doing this for her sick cousin—"

"Sheila?" He looked confused. "She's quite ill, but I fail to see how—"

Assumpta interrupted her. "She's ill because of these demons—"

"Exactly," Jo said, cutting off Assumpta before she accidentally propelled them into another argument. "The demons are causing her sickness, which is why the doctors are having a hard time diagnosing and curing her. We have the means to help her, and we hoped you would fulfill a small but important role tonight as we try to do so."

"Demons. *Witchcraft.*" Father Tony's entire demeanor changed to one of self-defeat. "Where did I go wrong with you, Assumpta?"

"It's not like that—"

"We'll talk when this is over." A changed seemed to come over him when uttered that statement. He stood tall again and straightened his shoulders—not indignant like he had been a moment ago, but resolved. His eyes were no longer friendly—or caring. "Or maybe we won't," he said.

There was silence in the store when Father Tony broke with Assumpta. Assumpta seemed to collapse in upon herself at that declaration.

He asked, "What is the plan for the necklace?"

"I've asked Saint Michael to take it tonight," Assumpta said in barely a whisper. She didn't look at Father Tony. And Jo knew she was regretting—probably for the thousandth time—that she hadn't let Saint Michael take it from her the first time he'd asked.

The priest looked around the store, searching. "Is he here now?"

Assumpta lifted her head, shaking it. "He hasn't answered my call."

Father Tony gave her a sharp look. "But he'll be here?"

"I'm certain he will." Jo interrupted Father Tony's interrogation. She had *known* it would be a bad thing to have him here, but she hadn't expected him to turn against Assumpta. She hoped they could work it out later. But now, she needed everyone present to be alert. She laid the demon necklace on a display bust, arranging the chain to lie flat on the short-piled velvet, and fussing with the large medallion that hung from it to buy herself a moment to think.

"*You've* spoken with Saint Michael?"

She knew he'd asked that to put her in her place. A pagan couldn't possibly have talked with a saint. Little did he know.

"Yes." She stared down her nose at Father Tony with what she hoped was a superior attitude. "He revealed himself to me as the god Mars in a dream. But I'm convinced of his favoritism toward Assumpta." Silently, she dared him to refute Mars was Michael. When this was over she'd lord it over him that both she and Assumpta had seen and conversed with the saint, and he, *a priest*, had not. Petty, she knew, but it was the best argument she had at the moment to prove they were more on the path to salvation than he was. They'd been favored by the divine, after all, and he had not. Would that argument open his heart back to Assumpta? She hoped so.

"Then we don't know that he'll be here," Father Tony said.

Jo took a deep cleansing breath of eucalyptus incense, glad she'd set it to burning. She held it for the count of three and let it out again, willing her own turmoil to be swept away as she exhaled. Immediately, she felt calmer. But she needed to dispel the rest of the destructive energy in the store before they continued. Something was bound to go wrong with the plan with this much negativity floating around.

"I know what you're thinking, Father," Assumpta said. "But, keep an open mind. *Please.* I believe in Jo. I'm convinced that what we're doing here is for the best. That's why I'm participating, and why I've contacted Saint Michael."

Jo broke in. "But I completely understand why you're having a hard time with this. And I wouldn't blame you if you decided not to stay, Father." She hoped he'd see the statement for what it was: a means to recuse himself from the situation without having to take a major stand he might later have to back down from. She sincerely hoped he'd take her up on the offer. Assumpta wouldn't be happy—but she wasn't going to be happy any way they sliced it at this point. Father Tony had already said too much. But his leaving would go a long way to clearing out the negativity in the store.

After a brief moment of silence, when it seemed that every one of them had been holding their breath, Father Tony said quietly, "I think I need to stay." Even though Jo had hoped he'd answer otherwise, his statement seemed to burst the rising tension. Everyone breathed at once. He said, "I can't condone what's going on, but I can be here to help if things get out of hand. I'll pray." He retrieved his small prayer book and turned to the pages on exorcism.

Jo set the bust with the artfully arranged medallion upon it onto the table on the far side of the carpeted area, just outside the reach of the demon trap.

Jo asked, "Is everyone ready?"

"Yes." Assumpta moved to her place behind the counter.

"Of course." Father Tony poured his bottle of holy water into one of Jo's small cauldron's and commandeered a long sprig of fresh rosemary from the plant on the counter. He dunked it into the holy water, where it would be ready if he needed it.

Jo nodded. "Then let's get this show started."

CHAPTER 30

ASSUMPTA UNLOCKED THE FRONT DOOR, THEN stepped behind the front counter and into the chalk circle with its multiple rings of protection. She was careful to stand in the exact center so she wouldn't accidentally obliterate the lines and foul the protective ward. She would stay here, in the midst of the circles' protection, while Jo performed the magic which would send the demons back to Hell.

She hated that Jo was the one in danger this time. Hated that it was because of her that Jo had been brought to this point. *It should be me facing the demons again*, she thought, *not Jo. It should be my life in danger.* She felt powerless—which was exactly the way the demons had intended it.

While Jo performed the dangerous magic, she would stand here and pray—not for help, but for protection for herself, Father Tony, and most importantly, Jo. Someone had to try to keep them all safe while Jo gathered the demons into their midst. She wasn't quite certain Father Tony would see to Jo's safety.

But before that, she would perform the formal ritual which would call Saint Michael and the other archangels to help them.

Ritual. Father Tony would give her grief for succumbing to *pagan* magic, and probably coerce her into attending daily confession for the next month. It would be like Lent all over again. But she would argue that *candle magic* was inherently Catholic. Didn't service begin with the lighting of candles? She'd never attended a function without seeing an acolyte light them prior. Father Tony might insist she was wrong, but she wouldn't give in. She couldn't.

Of course, the entire issue might be moot. Considering his earlier ire, she wasn't certain he was going to be speaking to her after this. Could he do that? Refuse to talk with her? She supposed she could write a letter to the diocese and tattle, but that would bring different problems. No, if he didn't want to talk with her, she wouldn't fight him. To use one of Jo's favorite phrases, she'd cross that bridge when she had to.

Assumpta made the sign of the cross, then reached for the first rosemary-dressed pillar candle that she and Jo had prepared—the one dedicated to Saint Michael. She said a quick Act of Contrition—more because of the meditative qualities of the prayer than contriteness—and so, more focused, placed the candle due north on the chalk circle and lit it, then whispered the prayer invoking the safety and help of the archangels.

"Michael—" Her voice caught, and she felt the tears rising in her throat. "I call upon you to watch from the north—"

Grief filled her again, and she sagged against the glass counter, closing her eyes and thinking about Michael for a moment. He had ignored all her pleas since she'd refused to give up the demon medallion. He'd been right—she should have given it over to him when he'd asked the first time. She'd admitted that—aloud and in prayer—to God *and* Saint Michael. But she hadn't heard a peep from him since.

Would he ignore her now? In her moment of need? Would he ignore Jo—for whom she really begged his help?

She repeated her plea to Michael, then gathering herself together, she reached for the second candle, whispering, "Uriel, I call upon you from the east." She placed the candle on the east side of the circle and lit the wick. The third candle she placed at the southern point of the circle, saying, "From the south, I call upon you, Raphael, to guard this circle and protect me—no, to protect Jo, Father Tony, me and any other innocents who may stray into this place of warfare. Please protect us from your fallen brethren." She settled the last candle on the western-most point of the chalk circle. "Gabriel, archangel of *His* armies, guard us—Jo, Father Tony and me—and anyone else who might stumble along—as Jo does battle against *His* foes who seek to do us and our family and friends harm." Assumpta lit the final candle, and nodded to Jo, who nodded back, and opened the demon book to a marked location.

Father Tony approached Assumpta, frowning at the dressed candles and their location on the pagan circles. "You said your part here tonight was to pray for her safety."

"I *am* praying for her safety. And *yours*."

Jo began speaking from the book, her words low and guttural, and Assumpta knew she had started chanting the banishment spell. Even though the demons hadn't arrived yet, Jo planned to draw the power to her now, and finish the spell when the demons were helplessly trapped in the Solomon Key. It was a matter of timing.

Assumpta turned to Father Tony. "Look, I know—"

Father Tony held up a hand to interrupt her. He was staring at Jo. "What language is Jo speaking?"

Assumpta shook her head. "I don't know." Which was the truth—she had no idea what language demons spoke. And telling Father Tony that Jo was speaking *demon language* would only make him angrier. Since it wouldn't help the situation, she kept that tidbit to herself. Lord help her if he found out. He'd only accuse her of lying by omission again.

"What book is she reading from?"

Assumpta shook her head. "You really don't want to know." There was no evading the answer to that one.

Father Tony turned back to Assumpta and frowned, then squinted his eyes and shielded them with an upraised hand. Immediately, he sank to his knees in supplication.

Saint Michael materialized to Assumpta's right, beside Uriel's candle, putting him between Father Tony and herself. He wore his holy armor and carried his flaming sword. Assumpta knew Michael's presence had filled Father Tony with the feeling of adoration, which had caused him to kneel.

Assumpta also knew Saint Michael hated that.

"Tell him to get up," Saint Michael said.

Father Tony saw Saint Michael only as a brilliant light. He was lucky Saint Michael allowed him even that. The archangel's presence went unnoticed by all but the few he deigned to reveal himself to. Assumpta leaned toward Father Tony and shook his shoulder. "Snap out of it," she said. "You have a job to do."

She'd felt the same compulsion to kneel the first few times Saint Michael had visited her, but repeated exposure to the saint had nearly driven it from her. There were times when he turned his full holy glory on her that she felt it again. But Saint Michael didn't take advantage of it.

Right now, she was profoundly grateful for his timely intervention—and elated to finally see him again. "I wasn't certain you would come. I see you're ready for battle." *Did he know something she didn't know—like how this was all going to play out?* Was more going to happen than she and Jo had planned? God, she hoped not.

"Isn't that what you called us for—battle?" the archangel asked.

"*Us?*" Assumpta looked beyond Saint Michael, but didn't see anything.

"Rafe, Uri, Gab..." He looked around the store, north, east and west—nodding at each compass point. "But you're not the only one who requires our help, so you need to get things moving if you want their protection—and mine. There are other people in need."

Assumpta continued scanning the room. "I don't see them." She had never actually seen the other angels, though she'd called on their protection before—and received it. Somehow, she thought it might be different this time, since Michael had taken to showing himself.

"They prefer to remain concealed," Saint Michael said. "And they're busy—you're lucky they're here at all." He held out his hand. "Do you have the medallion?"

Assumpta pointed to the bust across the room. "It's over there. You can have it after."

"After *what?*"

"After Jo captures the demons. It's being used as bait right now."

He quirked an eyebrow and took a step toward the small table the medallion sat on. "What's to stop me from just taking it?"

Stunned at the possibility, Assumpta simply stared at him. Then she pulled herself together. "Well—nothing, I suppose. But it would throw a major monkey wrench in tonight's affairs. Jo needs it right now to call the demons."

"Call the demons?" He cocked an ear in Jo's direction, and a frown furrowed his brow. He looked angry, no, furious. "How in Heaven's name did she obtain that book? Maybe you should fill me in on what you expect from me tonight—what you expect from all of us."

"So now you're listening?"

"I've always listened," Saint Michael said quietly. "You've just never opened your heart and given me the entire truth."

CHAPTER 31

ASSUMPTA LEANED AGAINST THE COUNTER, breathing in the soothing scent of rosemary while she considered where to begin telling Saint Michael about the plan. How much should she tell him? He was God's messenger...why didn't he already know about the plan for goodness sake? And then she remembered that once—in a fit of anger—Saint Michael had let slip that he wasn't always privy to the workings of the universe, even though he did His bidding.

Sometimes, angels—even archangels—worked on a need-to-know basis.

Assumpta had best start from the beginning, but make it fast.

She took a deep breath and filled him on the fact that Jo was dying, and about Sheila, and that the demons sought to make her miserable by torturing and killing her friends and family before finally coming for her—all because she possessed the medallion, and wouldn't give it to them.

"I told you—"

"Zip it," she said, holding up a hand to Saint Michael. "And forgive me, please, for my rudeness." Assumpta had gotten the *you'd better respect me* speech from Saint Michael more than once in the past. Hearing it right now wasn't going to make her mend her ways.

And she really didn't need to hear *I told you so* right now, either. She said less sharply, "You wanted to hear the plan, so I'm telling you the plan. Please listen."

Saint Michael frowned, shutting his mouth, but his eyes were stormy.

"You already know Jo is using the medallion as bait to get the demons here. What you don't know is that she targeted the specific demons trying to harm us, revealing to them that she now had possession of the medallion and telling them when and where it would be available. The rug in front of the table is hiding a demon trap.

"My part was to pray for you and your brothers to come and help us. Right now, Jo is chanting a spell which banishes demons from this plane. She'll refrain from speaking the last lines until the demons arrive and are trapped."

Saint Michael looked as though he would say something, but Assumpta held up her hand again, forestalling him. "The demons will have to cross the rug to get to the medallion. Once they're lured across the trap and held there, Jo will speak the final words of the spell, sending them back to Hell. Then, you may have the medallion."

"As long as everything goes to plan."

"Why wouldn't it?"

"Because demons are involved—and people," Saint Michael growled, smoothing back his tousled blond curls. His fingers seemed to pass right through his halo. "What's the plan for when things don't go according to plan?"

Assumpta swallowed hard, a lump suddenly in her throat. "Well—Father Tony is here to exorcise the demons if the trap and the spell don't work, and if that fails, there's you and the other angels."

"Then you'd better hope all goes according to plan."

"Why?"

"Because I have a feeling, if something goes wrong, that there won't be time enough for an exorcism. And the rules that govern our actions are fairly strict. Without a direct order, you know we can't step in to help unless there are extraordinary circumstances. And the demons know this, too."

"And how can we make certain that order comes?" Assumpta contemplated falling to her knees and begging God for help, now, before the demons arrived, realizing that she probably should have started from that point, rather than with calling the angels for protection. She crossed herself and bent one knee, sinking to the floor.

With a bleak look, Saint Michael lifted her by the elbow. "Jo has a better chance of gaining His attention than you right now. I told you not giving me the medallion when you had the opportunity was going to cost you. At least the small stain on your soul is not as bad as being demon-marked."

"I thought you'd told Jo I hadn't fallen from His grace?" The lump in Assumpta's throat seemed to grow massive, choking her.

"Fear not. It takes more than a single act of disobedience to fall from His grace. Let's just say you're not on His list of priorities right now."

"But if things should go all pear shaped—"

"Let's hope they don't."

CHAPTER 32

JO BLINKED, TURNING ON HER DEMON VISION, and looked around the shop. She let out a deep, relieved sigh, seeing very little to disturb her. She'd imagined the worst; with the wards dropped, all kinds of creepy-crawly things would invade. And some had. A few of the wormy bugs were inching across the bookshelves, and she saw tiny glowing eyes in two corners, which might have reminded her of kittens if she hadn't known better. Then, a ghost wandered through—a soldier with a bloody rag wrapped around his head, dressed in revolutionary garb. It breached the glass of the front door as if it didn't exist and walked through the store and out the back wall without deviating, passing through shelves, racks and merchandise.

All harmless things—for the moment.

She started chanting the spell that would send the demons back to Hell, binding the needed energies to the store, and herself, so that when the demons were assembled in the trap, she'd be ready. Once they were trapped, she need only speak the final few lines of the incantation to activate the spell and banish them.

It was a delicate process, and timing was key, for she could only keep the borrowed energy contained for so long before it would dissipate, and then she'd lose her chance to complete it. She could always begin the spell again, but she didn't want to run the risk of making a group of angry, trapped demons even angrier while she started over. And they might have friends they could call on to help. She didn't need an all-out demon war on her hands. She had to act quickly once everything was set in motion.

Saint Michael appeared, and she stumbled on a word of the spell. She stopped chanting and simply stared at him—with demon vision.

Gone was Mars, her pagan god. He looked to her as Assumpta had once described—blond and handsome. Clean shaven. Heavily muscled, but clad in holy—*glowing*—armor. The rounded tops of his enormous, snowy wings rose above his head; the tips nearly touched the ground. A gleaming, golden halo, tilted at a rakish angle, circled his brow, and he carried a flaming sword. His face was stern, and he looked ready for war. And he was staring at her with an angry look on his face. *Hell's bells. It was the demon book, wasn't it?*

But she couldn't think about his anger now. His *holy*, saintly glow took her off guard, entranced her, and she felt herself fumbling for the words of the demon spell, even as she looked at the page. She quickly read to the end of the line, the end of the stanza—a good stopping place for the moment—and felt compelled to look at Saint Michael again. When she looked back to the archangel, he seemed to glow even brighter with holy aura; she was suffused with a dual sense of murderous envy—and the overwhelming feeling of loss.

Then it dawned on her: she could see him *because* of the demon vision. And that's why he was Saint Michael, and not Mars. A glance around the room, and she saw the other archangels, too—Rafael, Uriel, Gabriel—all dressed in their holy, glowing armor. All prepared for battle. All staring at her with accusing eyes.

Pain swept over her, tears running down her face, and she knew she was experiencing the emotions of the *fallen* angels—the demons.

Jo blinked hard, blocking the demon vision, hoping to erase the demon feeling. It was simply too much, too large a burden, to think about at this crucial time. She caught herself feeling sorry for the demons—for herself. She could almost understand their antipathy to all that was good. *Almost.* Until she remembered they'd been privy to everything they would lose, and they chose their path anyway.

She took a deep, cleansing breath of eucalyptus. Saw Father Tony stand at the touch of Assumpta's hand, rising shakily to his feet. His face seemed a polar opposite of what her own must have looked like, espying Saint Michael with demon vision. She saw joy and inner peace, and wondered if Saint Michael had finally revealed himself to the priest.

She couldn't see Saint Michael anymore—though he must have been present. Without the demon vision, her sight was like anyone else's—unable to see either wicked *or* divine.

The shop bell rang and Jo tore her eyes away from them. Pournelle stood at the front door, glaring at her.

CHAPTER 33

J O STARED IN HORROR AT POURNELLE. WHY, OH why, did he have to show up *now*?

Her heart started thumping, and her head felt like it was going to explode.

She marked her place in the demon book, but didn't close it, laying it open on the small table beside the bust. She didn't need this—didn't need Pournelle—messing things up right now.

She didn't need him getting *hurt*.

"What are *you* doing here?" Father Tony asked, lifting his pectoral cross upward on its chain and thrusting it toward Pournelle, as if to ward him away. "Be gone."

"This again, holy man?" The exasperation was clear in the demon's voice. He sounded tired, weary of having to combat the priest yet again. "My beef is not with you tonight. Stand aside."

Father Tony grasped the rosemary springs resting in the holy water and whipped them over his head, flinging the blessed liquid in Pournelle's direction. Droplets rained down on him. Where the water landed, his suit coat shriveled and steamed. Small fires burst into flame on his exposed skin, which blackened and peeled away.

"I said, '*Stand aside*.'" Pournelle waved his hand, and Father Tony took two puppet-like steps to the left, out of Pournelle's way."

The demon approached Jo. "I'm here to see if the rumors are true." His words were curt. "Do you have the demon medallion?"

"Go away," Jo said, "It isn't safe here for you today." That was true. Even if he didn't step foot in the demon trap, there was no telling what would happen to him. Would the spell she wrought target him, too, even though he would be standing outside the trap? Would Saint Michael, or any of the other angels, attempt to send him back to Hell? He was in danger of Father Tony's exorcism rites, as well. She didn't want Pournelle hurt because of her.

"Today?" Father Tony hissed, lifting the sodden rosemary again. "What do you mean, *today?*"

They both ignored him until the fiery drops rained down again. The water felt cool on Jo's heated face, but Pournelle burned. He snapped his fingers and the rosemary stems in Father Tony's hand burst into flames. Father Tony dropped them to the floor and stepped on them, extinguishing the fire.

Pournelle snapped his fingers again, and his suit was once more pristine. The skin on his hands and face remained burned, buy she could see it slowly healing. He gave Jo a sharp look. "So you do have it."

She nodded.

"How did you come by it?"

She didn't answer, but her eyes slid to Assumpta's.

Pournelle turned to her. "You've had the medallion—for how long?" He frowned. "Have you—"

"Never!" Assumpta said. "I've never used it against you—never even considered using it against you."

"And with all your talk of *good will?* You'll pardon me if I can't quite find it in myself to believe you about that."

"She speaks the truth." Jo stepped away from the small table— and the medallion. Hoping to put herself between it and Pournelle—if things came to that.

"You were with her every second that she had it?" Pournelle

snapped. "You know exactly how she's used it?" His eyes bored into hers. "Would you bet your life on it?"

Jo felt as if she'd been physically stuck. "Well, no, but—"

"Save it." Pournelle said. He sidestepped her, and approached the table with the bust. "I want to examine it. I want to hold it in my hands—if just for a moment."

"Stop!" Assumpta yelled from behind the counter. "Don't move any closer. The rug—"

Pournelle stopped. He looked at her. Then he looked down at the expensive rug. He knelt and lifted the corner, revealing the chalk lines of the Solomon's Key. He gave Jo a hateful look and circumvented the sigil, walking around the perimeter of the carpet to the small table Jo had set the bust upon. He bent to examine it, hands behind his back, but Jo could see them twitching and knew Pournelle itched to pick up the medallion—to feel its power for himself. He turned back to Jo. "You aim to trap them. You're going to try to send them back to Hell."

She nodded.

Next to Assumpta, Father Tony was muttering under his breath. Pournelle caught his eye. "And you—do you plan to *exorcise* them?"

Father Tony didn't answer, still muttering words—probably praying—under his breath. She hoped he wasn't trying to exorcise Pournelle.

Jo replied. "Yes—if it comes to that. The trap will catch them, and I'm using a banishment spell from *the book you gave* me—" She didn't dare say *demon* book in Father Tony's presence. "—to send them back to Hell."

Pournelle said, "You won't have enough time—even with your avenging army." He made a sweeping gesture with his hand, encompassing the entire store, and Jo wondered if he could see Saint Michael and the other angels. *Why hadn't they tried to stop him?*

"You need to get rid of the medallion before the *others* arrive. You can be certain there will be more here than even your angelic host can handle. Your only option is to get rid of the lure." He turned back to the necklace. "I can get rid of it for you."

"I realize it's dangerous," Jo said. "But without bait for the trap, I'll never get the demons here. And then I'll never be able to break the curse on me—or Sheila."

"There's always another way," Pournelle said. "You can't chance letting a demon get the medallion."

"I've no intention of that. Saint Michael will claim it before any of the demons do," Jo said.

"That's a lot of moving pieces." Pournelle folded his arms across his chest. "Are you sure you can make it all work?" He turned and surveyed the set up again. "What if you can't—and a demon gets to the medallion? What is your fallback, in case your plan fails?"

Jo was calculating the time in her head, trying to figure out how many minutes had passed, and how many more could slide before she needed to start chanting the banishment spell again. She didn't have time to argue with Pournelle. "It can't fail," she said.

"You mean you don't want it to fail."

"Of course I don't! Failure means I die."

Pournelle's face smoothed out, his look almost sorrowful. "Trust me when I tell you there are things worse than death."

The bell rang over the door and Chip, the college-student demon, walked in. One hand was shoved innocuously into his jean's pocket, and his usual cheery smile was plastered on his face.

A dull thud pounded in her chest as Jo realized all the plans she'd set in motion were finally in action.

Chapter 34

IT MUST BE STRANGE FOR CHIP, JO THOUGHT, WHEN he walked into the store, all eyes pointing in his direction. The smile on his face faded, and she knew he had to feel the tension in the air. But could he see the angels in the room? Maybe not, or he'd have walked right back out again. Then again, maybe he did—and he simply ignored them because he figured that no one else knew they were there.

Maybe.

Or, maybe he was simply willing to risk everything for the demon medallion, and the power he could wield if he obtained it.

Chip looked around the store, zeroing in on the medallion on the table far across the room, then casually looked away as if it didn't mean anything. He stopped at the incense, then moved on to look at a few candles, and finally walked to the athame display in the back of the room. The ceremonial knives weren't weapons, but certainly could be employed as such. Did Chip plan on using one? Jo's heart beat a little harder. He lifted a decorative knife from a stand, hefted it, then replaced it—before taking another step closer to the medallion.

Jo's eyesight was deteriorating—or should she consider it improving? She no longer needed the glasses to see that Chip wasn't human. And even without *blinking* on her demon sight, she could see the vaguest outline of a demon under Chip's supernatural glamour. The wings of his much larger demon form looked ghost-like and ethereal protruding from his shoulder blades. On his forehead, the curling horns were shadows still, faint impressions of what they really were. She shivered. Did she really want to see things like that all the time?

Jo forced a smile. "Hi, Chip. Can I help you with anything?" She hoped she sounded more relaxed than she felt. She willed her thumping heart to return to normal.

The *young man* gave her his usual smile. "Not really." He shrugged and walked toward the medallion. "Just killing some time before class, as usual." His smile growing larger, and he edged closer to the small display table. "That's cool-looking. New merchandise?"

Jo shook her head. Was he deliberately playing dumb? Maybe he didn't think she knew what she had in her possession. "Not so much, Chip. I got that at a recent estate sale and decided it wasn't for me. Do you want to take a closer look?"

"Could I? Maybe my girlfriend would like it," he said, stepping onto the carpet.

Gotcha! Jo thought. And he didn't even realize it. She liked that kind of spell.

"Is it okay if I try it on?" His toothy, college-boy grin might have fooled her—had fooled her in the past—but no longer. Jo knew him for what he really was.

"I thought it was for your girlfriend," she said, ribbing him a little, just as she always had before she realized Chip was a demon. It seemed easier to act as though everything were *status quo* until the last possible moment. There was no need to poke the bear; he'd get plenty angry on his own later.

"Well...if I like it enough," he said, still grinning, "then maybe it will be for me." Jo held her breath for just a second. One more step and Chip would realize that he was caught.

There was a scrape of the door at the top of her private stairs, and both of them turned to look.

No one should be upstairs.

But the door swung open, and a female demon in a navy blue suit and matching heels came down the stairs toward Jo. She looked like a beautiful, confident attorney—with stunning Mediterranean looks, her dark, glossy hair pulled up in a bun. Her stylish suit rivaled Pournelle's. She carried a burgundy-colored, hard-sided briefcase and smiled smugly. Jo just stared, her stomach plummeting. She hadn't expected this. The slow thump of her heart that started when Chip had walked in, changed to a rapid, staccato beat.

The demon's power had to be very strong, unlike Chip's, Jo thought, because it was hiding its natural shape well. Jo could only see the vaguest outline of wings over the demon's head, and no hint of horns or fangs at all. If she hadn't have been staring so intently at the *woman*, Jo wouldn't have seen a thing.

"Don't look so surprised, dear," the demon said, marching down the stairs toward Jo, the heels of her shoes striking loudly on the wooden treads. "You might have dropped the wards, but you didn't close the curtain. I saw your cavalry from the sidewalk—not that I expect them to do anything. *Spiritual support*—" the demon said the words sharply, her human mouth twisting as if the phrase tasted bad, "is about all angels are good for these days." She paused on the last step, resting her hand on the newel post and surveying the layout. "I've skipped walking your gauntlet, and now I'm on this side of the room, closest to the medallion, and furthest away from anything else you might have planned."

Out of the corner of her eye, Jo saw Pournelle turn away from the demon, making a show of looking over the nearby candles, as if he didn't want her to see him, and then he slowly made his way to the front of the store. The demon either missed him, or considered him beneath her notice—effectively discounting Pournelle.

She stepped down off the final stair and into the room, putting her free hand on one hip and squaring her shoulders. "In the interest of time, I suggest we forgo whatever you've got planned and cut to the chase. So, here's what I'm offering—"

"If anyone is going to offer Jo anything, it's me," Chip said. Gone was the college-boy demeanor. He still looked like a young man—but the voice was deeper, harder—no longer easy-going. "The medallion is mine. I was here first."

The newcomer looked Chip up and down, dismissing him. "Timing certainly has its place in business, but I'm certain Ms. Byrne will see that since you have so little to bargain with, you're a non-player in this transaction."

"I was hand-picked by Adrian as the Successor."

Jo froze. Chip was Adrian's successor? She stared at him, trying to determine if Chip was telling the truth. Was it possible? No, he had to be bluffing—there was Caroline's baby to consider. Caroline and Adrian's baby.

The she-demon laughed. "But Adrian no longer *exists*. And since he didn't see to the succession before his untimely demise, what Adrian wanted no longer matters." The demon raised the briefcase horizontally, unsnapped the clasps and opened it up for Jo to see the contents. "We're prepared to pay you handsomely for the medallion. There's five-hundred-thousand dollars here—enough to pay off your mortgage and do some renovations if you desire."

CHAPTER 35

JO WAS STUNNED. IF ONLY SHE WERE WILLING TO part with the medallion—but it wasn't hers to give. Some days she cursed herself for not having a more mercenary personality. The things she could do with that kind of cash! Yes, she could pay off the mortgage on the apartment upstairs and maybe do some renovations. But jeez, she'd like to tuck away most of it for retirement. *Early* retirement. Days like today had her thinking about the possibility of it more and more.

The demon closed and locked the briefcase, then looked at her delicate, diamond-studded wristwatch. "You've got ten minutes to decide."

Jo cleared her throat. She didn't need to be a genius to hear the other half of the demon's unspoken threat. *If you don't decide* yes, *we'll take the matter out of your hands.* Jo knew what that meant.

"So, let me get this straight," Jo said, trying to buy some time. "I get the money, you get the medallion, and we each go our merry way—never to meet again?"

"That's right," the demon said.

"No—" Chip disagreed.

Jo ignored him. *Think,* she told herself. *Think. Was there a way out of this situation without anyone or anything getting hurt?* With the original plan gone awry, she needed a new one. And she needed some time to formulate it, so she continued to talk. "What about lifting all spells on Assumpta's family and friends? And we'll need some kind of guarantee that all of them will be protected in the future." She picked up the medallion, clasping the round, brass casing in her palm and letting the thick chain dangle over the back of her hand. "And some kind of truce in Baltimore and the surrounding area." *Could I actually make a deal with this demon? No,* she thought, *even if it agreed to all my requests, I couldn't trust it to follow through—*

"Don't bargain with the enemy!" Father Tony said, approaching them. "Demons are evil incarnate. You can't trust them—they spew nothing but lies."

"Don't do it," Assumpta pleaded from her place behind the counter.

Jo turned to include both the priest and Assumpta in the conversation. She smiled broadly, then winked, hoping they would catch the signal. She said, "But this may be the solution we've all been looking for. We can sign an *equitable* contract that demons are *so very fond of...*" She lingered on the words, playing out the last few, and emphasizing the demon partiality for contracts. Assumpta—who'd been offered several demonic bargains of her own in the last year— seemed to catch her hint, but she wasn't certain about Father Tony. "I think we should consider it."

"Demand that no demons be allowed to enter your store again," Assumpta said. She was smoothing her hands across the counter— *reaching for a weapon?*—but looking at Jo. She nodded almost imperceptibly, and Jo knew she'd understood.

"Father Tony?" Jo gave him her full attention. "Would you like the demons to stay out of your church? The rectory?" The questions angered him, as Jo knew they would. Blood colored his face red, and she was certain she could see him starting to shake. She used his delay in responding to look for a weapon of her own.

"Madness!" Father Tony finally sputtered.

The demon smiled tightly and placed the briefcase on the floor. She reached into her left jacket pocket and pulled out a folded piece of paper. "We're prepared to deal if the money by itself isn't good enough." A pen appeared in her other hand. "All I need is your signature, Jo."

"You can't do this," Chip said, low, guttural. "*I* was here first. *I* staked my claim. The medallion is *mine*."

The other demon frowned. "I told you not to challenge me on this, Chip. Walk away now, and I'll let you live when I'm in charge."

"That'll never happen," Chip said, suddenly sprinting for the medallion. Jo froze. She didn't know if he'd meant that the demon wouldn't let him live, or that she would never be in charge. But the thought was fleeting—and moot.

Father Tony yelled, "No!" and also charged toward Jo.

Chip was faster, but he was already caught in the trap of the Solomon's Key. When he reached the edge of the carpet, it was as though he slammed into a brick wall. He bounced off hard and hit the floor while Father Tony reached Jo and wrestled the medallion from her. "This cannot fall into the hands of a demon," he said. "I can protect it."

"God dammit!" Chip yelled, rubbing his forehead and sitting up. He scrambled to his feet and paced the length of the carpet, discovering the boundaries of the demon trap like a caged tiger.

"Blasphemer!" Father Tony cried, clutching the thick links of the medallion's chain close to his chest with his left hand, the medallion hanging down awkwardly and knocking against his pectoral cross. "This is mine now—" He skirted the edge of the rug, raised the pectoral cross at the female demon and backed away. "Be gone."

"Be gone?" She crossed her arms over her chest and laughed. "Did you really think that would work?" Then, she dropped all pretense of humanity, taking on her true demon form, growing in height and girth. Her skin darkened to the distinctly demonic mottled black-and-red; scissor-like talons appeared at the ends of her fingers. Her mouth was all snout with razor-sharp teeth and thick lips pushed back in a permanent snarl. The demon hulked over them, greater than six feet tall, with wings even higher, yet large enough to brush the ground. No trace of the human woman remained.

The demon scowled and unfurled her wings, slapping an iron cauldron across the room where it banged against the front counter with a hollow ring. Books and herbs and candles were knocked to the floor as the wings rose up and up, over the demon's head—a bold, leathery mantle. She stepped toward Father Tony. Her eyes bored into his, like a hypnotist's might, Jo thought. Her words were soft, cajoling, still in the feminine, human voice, "Why don't you just hand over the medallion?" She licked her lips with a black, forked tongue, then held out a clawed hand to the priest. "I'll let you live if you rest it in my hand."

It was the same deal the demon had offered to Chip, and Jo couldn't help but wonder how often the threat had worked with others—both demon and human. The demon was clearly accustomed to getting what she wanted.

Father Tony took another step backward, looking suddenly panicked. He turned his head first to the right, then to the left, trying, apparently, to determine which way might offer the easiest path away from the demon. "No." He whispered, barely pushing the word beyond his teeth. Then, "*No.*" Stronger, louder. Father Tony stood taller, clearly realizing there was no place to go. He would face down this demon.

Keeping the medallion firmly gripped in one hand, Father Tony grasped his pectoral cross with the other, raising it upward and outward toward the demon. He began chanting low, under his breath.

The demon roared, beating her leathery, muscled chest. She flung her arms wide. Orange flames appeared in the palms of her clawed hands, then licked upward to her elbows and shoulders. She sprang on Father Tony, leaping into the air and beating her wings once, twice, to propel herself forward, closing the distance between them. Father Tony released his hold on the cross and grasped the medallion, protecting it with two hands. He turned away, shielding it from the demon's reach.

The demon wrapped its blazing arms around the priest, knocking them both to the floor, setting Father Tony's robes on fire. Father Tony screamed as they tumbled to the ground, flames licking at his skin. The fall separated them. The priest rolled away from the demon, smothering the Hellish fire beneath him, and retreating from the danger. He stood.

Jo took a deep breath. It was just the opening she had been looking for—even if it hadn't occurred as she might have liked it. She grabbed the demon book, found the last lines of the banishment spell, and said them aloud.

Nothing happened.

"*Damn, damn, damn.*" Had she said the words incorrectly? She'd practiced this aloud a dozen or more times! She said the words again, slowly and carefully, working hard not to trip over the unfamiliar syllables. Again, nothing happened.

"No!" Chip said again, retreating backward into the cage of the Solomon's Key. "You can't do this," he yelled at Jo. He turned to the larger demon. "How does she know our language? Our spells? How can this be?"

The she-demon slowly picked herself up from the floor and stalked toward Father Tony. "She has the medallion. She has a book. Adrian's necklace—and I suspect Adrian's book. Having one would have made it easy to come by the other. The language would have come naturally."

Too much time had passed since she started the original spell, Jo realized. It only seemed like moments, with everything happening so fast. She started chanting the banishment spell again, this time from the beginning. If she could recite it fast enough, maybe she could save Father Tony.

"No!" Chip screamed. He ran to the edge of his limits, beating against the invisible wall imprisoning him. His face was in agony. "Not that. Never that. I surrender my rights to the medallion. I'll leave here and never return." His voice was pleading. "Don't send me into oblivion."

The other demon looked over her shoulder and halted briefly, as if making a decision. Jo imagined her thinking: *Who can I get to first—the mewling priest who holds the key to my power in his hands, or the upstart witch who thinks she can best me?*

Jo hardened her heart.

If she didn't know any better, the sight of a young college student begging her to stop might have given her pause. As it was, it was Pournelle—stricken faced, who turned to her and mouthed, "Don't—" which made her hesitate. She'd forgotten he was there. The spell would annihilate him, too.

Time seemed to stand still.

The demon made her decision, turning back to Father Tony and slashing at him with clawed hands. Father Tony backed away from the sharpened talons. The demon struck out again—this time connecting, ripping Father Tony's robes and slicing through to his ribs. Father Tony screamed. The smell of burning silk filled the air, and blood ran in small rivulets from the priest's wounds.

Jo started chanting again. Fast.

Giving Jo a sad look, Pournelle raised his fingers and snapped. Nothing happened. A look of shock crossed his face. Jo felt the surprise in her gut. Still, she continued chanting. Chip whimpered in his cage. The female demon roared and scuttled forward toward the priest, whipping her hands like sabers. Father Tony continued to back up, until he couldn't retreat any farther.

Pournelle ran for the front door, yanked it open, and left.

Backed into a corner, Father Tony raised the medallion over his head and dropped it around his neck.

CHAPTER 36

"N O!" THE DIRECTIVE ECHOED THROUGH THE room like a clap of thunder.

Jo wasn't certain if it was she or Assumpta who had shouted it. It may have even been the demon, or Chip—or Saint Michael. Maybe all of them.

Father Tony squeezed his eyes tightly closed, his face contorted with obvious pain. He raised his hands to his ears and pressed them tightly, as if trying to block an excruciatingly loud noise. Jo heard nothing, yet it was clear that Father Tony struggled with something. Did the medallion wage war against him? Or was it his own conscience that seemed to be causing him such pain?

Brief seconds later, Father Tony's eyes sprang open. He dropped his hands. The lines in his face smoothed, his eyes appeared vacant, unfocused, and Jo knew—*knew in her heart*—that the body of Father Tony stood in front of her, but not the spirit. The medallion used Father Tony like a puppet.

"Back off," the demon Father Tony said. His voice was deeper, softer, almost a growl—an evil parody of how he must sound on the pulpit. Jo's stomach plummeted, as she realized how bad the situation was, and cursed herself that she had never considered the possibility that things might get out of hand like this. She'd been so naive.

Father Tony's cassock smoked where his pectoral cross lay. He yanked the cross from his neck, the skin of his palm and his neck sizzling where it touched the blessed metal. The odor of burnt flesh fouled the air. He flung it away from him, his hand still burning, then patted the fire out on his hip and gazed around the store, taking in the situation.

The large, winged demon backed away from Father Tony. She extinguished the remainder of her fire, knelt before the priest, and bowed. "I am at your service."

"No, no, no, no, no..." Chip whimpered in his cage, he walked back and forth, back and forth, testing the limits of the Solomon's Key. In a move certainly born of desperation, Chip fell to his knees and peeled back the corner of the carpet. But before he could even try to wipe away the lines—which Jo knew he couldn't possibly do—Father Tony raised a hand toward him and uttered a single word.

Chip exploded—splattering black-and-red blood and gore everywhere.

Assumpta screamed and dipped behind the front counter.

Jo ducked and covered her head with the demon spell book as bits of Chip—ravaged and bloody—rained down upon her and elsewhere throughout the store. Heart thumping so hard, she was certain it would pound its way out of her chest, Jo took a deep breath and whispered to herself. "Courage." *Hope isn't lost*, she thought. *If it were, surely the angels would get involved.* She took a deep, calming breath. *I can still make this right.*

The kneeling she-demon hung her head lower, folded her wings tighter to her back, making herself as unobtrusive as possible.

Father Tony—the *demon* Father Tony—turned in her direction and raised a hand to caress her ridged, curved horns. He smiled benignly, as a father might smile down upon a child. Then Father Tony moved his hand to her beefy shoulder and patted the demon, bending at the waist and saying a few low words in what must have been the demon language. Even though Jo had been studying the language for a while now, she had no idea what Father Tony said. But the demon shook out its wings and neatly refolded them, all the while nodding its head, as if agreeing to something. They seemed fixed in conversation. Could she escape their notice?

Jo wiped the demon blood from her eyes and stood slowly, not wanting to draw attention to herself, watching Father Tony and the other demon, in case they saw her and reacted. She moved to the glass counter and laid the demon book on top. When Assumpta started to rise, Jo motioned for her to stay down. Jo started chanting again—the demon banishment spell—in a mere whisper of words, so as not to alert the winged demon and Father Tony. Even though she knew much of the spell by heart at this point, she read directly from the book, not wanting to accidentally miss something. She swallowed. *I have to get this right.*

The air in the store grew thick with power, and she could feel the demon magic pulsing through her—along with nausea. She was going to be sick again with this much evil power coursing through her body. Jo swallowed hard, trying to keep the bile down, and continued.

Finally, she reached the critical point of the spell, the pause before the last two lines, and looked up at Father Tony. He was smiling at her—and not in a good way. Like he'd been waiting for her to get this far. Maybe he had. How could she be so stupid to think that a spell of such massive power would go unnoticed?

Quickly, she tried to spit out the last two lines.

Father Tony chuckled, and lifted his left hand, palm facing toward her and made a quick circular motion with his wrist. Again, he uttered words in the demon language Jo didn't understand. She choked, coughing, and choked again. Each time she tried to speak the final words of the banishment spell, she coughed, making it impossible for her to continue.

She stopped trying, because any more of this and she'd throw up.

But why hadn't he just killed her as he had killed Chip?

Her mind rattled off the reasons. *Because he needs me alive.*

Because it doesn't matter if I remain alive—since the demons are now in possession of the amulet. Because I'm a dead woman anyway, since I'm afflicted by the demon death-curse...

But did the demon who possessed Father Tony know about her scarab necklace? That she would remain alive until the demon who cast the death spell is dead? Did that play, or not play, into its plan?

All or none of these things could be right, she thought. Maybe the demon that possessed Father Tony chose not to kill any of them because it feared retribution from the angels.

Father Tony pushed aside the kneeling demon and stalked toward her, a look of thoughtful intent on his face. "You're putting up a good fight, Jo. I'm enjoying it. But the time has come to finish this. I've accomplished what I set out to do..."

What I set out to do? What could it mean? What could it have possibly *set out to do?*

And then she noticed it. She gasped.

Inky tendrils of smoke rose up from the center of the medallion resting on Father Tony's chest. The smoke coalesced, tightened into thicker strands, then stretched up and out, winding their way through the heavy links of the chain which held the medallion around Father Tony's neck.

Father Tony suddenly grasped his forehead and groaned. His eyes focused—*really focused*—on Jo. And when he spoke, the voice was his own. "What's going on...?" He looked around the store in confusion. "How did I get here? The pain—"

The smoky tendrils around his chest grew and magnified, crossed over one another and crossed again, twisting and winding themselves into a more dense shape. And as Jo watched, the shape took on a tiny, humanoid form, a head and arms bent at the elbow, attempting to wriggle its hips from the center of the medallion. The medallion had imprisoned a demon—and that demon was trying to flee. Jo had to stop it.

She looked around for something—anything—which might prevent the tiny, powerful demon from escaping the medallion.

What kind of foul deeds must a demon perform to be incarcerated by its brethren? Surely they would applaud the worst of the worst—not condemn them? Maybe, the demon was not culpable at all. Maybe it deserved to be set free.

Perhaps it only did the bidding of others because it was *bound by the medallion* to do so.

Jo felt a momentary pang of regret for the creature, but then she steeled herself. If its own kind had imprisoned it, it must be for a very good reason. Then another thought hit her: maybe the demons hadn't wanted the medallion for the power it could bring them. Maybe they wanted the medallion to make certain the demon inside never escaped.

But she had no time to dwell on *maybe* and *what-ifs.*

She reached for the spray Assumpta had used to bless the archangel's candles—holy water, consecrated salt and rosemary. She spritzed the tiny shadow escaping from the medallion. The cone-shaped mist of water reached as high as Father Tony's forehead, and as low as the rope cincture at his waist.

The demon screeched and retreated back into the medallion.

Father Tony's stare became vacant again, and then he screamed and rubbed his face where the holy water burned him, smearing blood and tearing off bits of tender flesh along with crisp, burned skin. His cincture—also caught in the spray of the holy water—melted away where the water touched—and fell to the floor, leaving his robes hanging loose at the waist.

She had hoped the three-times-blessed water would do more to harm the tiny demon—like set it on fire, or send it fleeing back to the depths of Hell. *No such luck.* But as long as she stood as a sentinel in front of the medallion and sprayed the demon whenever it tried to emerge, she could keep in contained.

Hissing, it poked its head out of the medallion, again, turning its face toward her. Its tiny eyes, aflame, stared back at her with malevolence. It flung an arm toward her, fingers splayed in her direction, uttering beneath its breath.

Jo sprayed again, catching him in mid spell. The demon shrank back from the blast of water, retreating back into the necklace. Father Tony screamed, small droplets of blood appearing on his face. He raised a hand to his eyes and wiped, mixing blood with holy water and singeing his face more in the process. Clearly, the water did more damage to Father Tony than the demon when the demon was in full possession of the priest.

She couldn't let the little demon escape—and she couldn't keep hurting Father Tony. But how was she supposed to get the medallion from around his neck?

Jo realized with a sinking feeling what she had to do. If she wanted to stop the demon, she had to immobilize Father Tony. It was the only way she was going to get the medallion—and the demon—away from him. But if the large winged she-demon hadn't been able to best Father Tony, how could she possibly do so—especially when he was possessed by a powerful demon?

I don't stand a chance, she thought. *But he no longer has his cross or holy water. He can't touch them with the demon possessing him. Maybe it was possible...*

She had to try. She had to take down Father Tony even if it meant outright killing him. And she could use some help.

How could she convey that to Assumpta without the demon realizing it? And would Assumpta help her kill Father Tony—her childhood mentor—if it came to that? It seemed unlikely, and yet, she had to try.

Jo tried to catch Assumpta's eye and realized that Assumpta had her own plan. A cool rain fell across the room—rosemary scented *holy* rain. Assumpta held the cauldron of holy water Father Tony had prepared earlier. She dipped the rosemary fronds into the water and flung them toward Father Tony again.

The droplets struck Father Tony and the still-kneeling she-demon, burning through Father Tony's robes to his bare skin. Blood ran down his face in tiny rivulets, and he rubbed at them, spreading the holy water and doing more damage. It flayed the black-and-red mottled skin of the demon, leaving bits of skin hanging as thick, black blood seeped from the multiple small wounds. Both roared in pain.

Assumpta dipped the rosemary branches into the holy water again and flung more droplets in their direction. The water cooled Jo, just as it burned the demons, taking away some of the nausea she felt from working the demon spells.

Jo twisted the spout of the spray bottle to tighten the flow of water, then sent a stream of her own blessed water directly at the medallion. She missed, hitting Father Tony square in the chest, burning through his robes and down to his flesh. He howled, face contorted in pain.

She sprayed again.

Assumpta let loose with another barrage of holy water.

The she-demon stood and unfurled her wings, knocking books and candles and incense off shelves. She beat her wings once, twice, leapt over Father Tony and Jo, and headed straight for Assumpta—who, Jo assumed—it considered a bigger threat by raining down holy water.

And *crap*, Assumpta no longer stood in her circles of protection, but to the left of the counter, where she'd had a better line of vision for the holy water salvo.

The demon's wing tips swept across the edge of the counter, knocking over the cash register and the samovar, spilling hot water across the waxed paper still full of cut rosemary leaves. The she-demon roared, and reached out to Assumpta.

In the blink of an eye, an angel stepped between them.

Uriel, Jo thought, since he had come from the north.

Where Saint Michael was blond and fair, Uriel was dark and stoic. His eyes gleamed with holy vengeance, and he looked as pitiless as any demon. He raised his hand and touched the winged demon on the forehead.

Jo ducked, thinking the demon would explode the same as Chip. Instead, the demon plummeted to the floor, screaming, Uriel's hand still upon her brow.

The demon writhed, her wings curling up at the edges and steaming. Her mouth opened and closed, opened and closed, her screams getting weaker and weaker. Serrated teeth ground against one another, then bit down into the leathery flesh of her black-and-red tongue. Blood seeped over her thick lips, running down over her protracted jaw and dripping onto the floor.

Uriel grabbed her horns in both hands, twisting the demon's neck in a painful angle. Smoke roiled up from where the angel touched the bony protuberances. At once, the horns caught fire. A white-hot blaze of holy flame incinerated them with other-worldly haste. The demon continued to scream.

"Enough!" Saint Michael shouted.

Uriel thrust the demon away from him with a disgusted push, his face a mask of resigned vengeance—as though he took no pleasure in the work, only sought to do it as best he could—while inflicting as much pain as possible.

He reached to his hip and pulled out a fiery sword. Jo blinked. It hadn't been there a moment ago—or maybe it just hadn't been a blazing fury a moment ago. Uriel lifted the sword and cleaved the she-demon in two, slicing through bone and sinew and wing. A normal sword might have required hacking; Uriel's melted through the tough, leathery skin without effort.

Jo gasped, her feet suddenly leaden as she was held in place. She dropped the spray bottle.

Her feet warmed, then burned, and then the fiery sensation moved upward to her knees, her ankles, her hips—leaving a cool sensation as it passed. The burn moved upward through her belly, her chest, her neck and face, and finally out the top of her head with a blazing pain—and then sudden coolness and relief. The sensation even passed through the tips of her spiky black hair, burning then cooling, before dissipating.

She stumbled, smiling, and caught herself on the edge of the counter. The death spell—she was certain of it—was utterly broken—

the tendrils that bound her to the demon were not just severed, but eradicated. She would live.

And the she-demon was dead. Its black-and-red blood, thick and viscous, seeped to the floor, burning the finish from the hardwood and eating through the carpeting like acid with small puffs of smoke. The odors of rotten meat and burned nylon warred with each other.

Uriel sheathed his sword, knelt once more, and touched both halves of the body simultaneously. The body *imploded*, shriveling upon itself. Its edges rolled and curled. The bone softened, and then compacted. Skin shrunk and tightened around the mass until all that was left were two black-and-garnet lumps resembling cooling lava, each the size of a small shoe box.

Father Tony—the real Father Tony—stood frozen, watching, his expression both confused and horrified.

The tiny demon was working itself out of the medallion again, only its knees and feet remained. Jo lunged for the spray bottle at her feet. She grabbed it, aimed for the medallion, and pulled the trigger handle. A fine stream of rosemary-scented water hit the medallion squarely, splashing the demon—and then petered out.

But it was enough to scare off the demon, apparently.

It hunkered back into the necklace. The light in Father Tony's eyes died as the demon took over. He charged at Jo.

Jo tossed away the useless spray bottle and gazed around for another weapon. The counter had been swept nearly clean by the winged demon, leaving a pool of cooling water, sodden wax paper and rosemary petals...and scissors—the ones she and Assumpta had used to cut the rosemary.

Father Tony slammed into Jo, forcing the hard, glass edge of the counter into her spine. Leaning into her, he wrapped his fingers around her neck and squeezed.

Acute pain ravaged her throat. She fumbled blindly for the scissors.

Father Tony pressed his thumbs harder—and Jo's fingers curled around the brass handles. She tightened her grip, tensed her muscles, then plunged the scissors into Father Tony's shoulder.

The scissors seared his skin, almost cauterizing the wound, since they'd been splashed in holy water. A small tendril of smoke curled up from Father Tony's singed garments. A burnt-flesh odor assailed her.

Jo gave the scissors a good twist, pushing them in deeper into Father Tony's shoulder and using all the leverage she had to knock him off balance. He screamed and fell to his knees, clutching his shoulder. Jo bent and picked up the heavy iron cauldron still lying near the base of the counter. "Please don't let me kill him," she prayed, and swung it hard against Father Tony's head.

He collapsed to the floor.

CHAPTER 37

THERE WAS COMPLETE AND TOTAL SILENCE IN the store.

Smoke eddied up from the carpet covering the demon trap. Father Tony lay crumpled on the floor, the scissors still sticking out of his shoulder, blood staining his white robes—the red patch growing larger and larger as the minutes passed. Around his neck were red, blistered scorch marks where the demon medallion had touched. His hand still bore the burn of the pectoral cross.

Jo took deep breaths and rubbed her throat, still recovering from Father Tony's attack. She was going to need tea—and the damned samovar had been pitched over. It would be the first thing she fixed when everyone was gone.

Assumpta ran to Father Tony, felt for a pulse, then chafed his uninjured hand. "Call 9-1-1!" she said, then urging Father Tony, "Wake up! Wake up."

He remained motionless.

Jo reached for the phone and called the paramedics.

Saint Michael knelt beside the priest. He took the medallion from Father Tony's neck, and set it on the floor, one booted foot pressed on the top of the jeweled necklace as if he thought the imprisoned demon might escape—or that the medallion might go running off on its own. Grim faced, he grasped the brass-handled scissors and pulled them from Father Tony's shoulder, then laid his palm gently on the wound. His expression darkened. "Rafe—"

Archangel Rafael approached and knelt, placing both hands on Father Tony's injury, his white-blond curls falling into his face as he bowed his head. Jo couldn't see around his hands to the bloodstained cloth, but the bloody stain on his robes stopped growing, and she imagined the wound knitting itself together. Rafael moved his hands to the priest's head, cradling it in his palms. The blisters and burns on Father Tony's face and arms disappeared, melting away as if they'd never been.

Jo guessed that he'd taken care of the lump she'd inflicted with the cauldron, as well. Finally, Rafael held Father Tony's burned hand in his own. Jo watched as the worst of the burned skin melted away from Father Tony's palm and fingers, leaving the faintest of scars. "In time, he'll be okay," Rafael said. His voice was certain and low, filled with assurance—a healer's voice.

"You can't erase it all?" Assumpta asked.

"All of the physical scars?" Rafael nodded. "I can."

"Then why don't you?" Jo retrieved the bloody scissors from the floor and dropped them back onto the counter.

"So he knows he didn't dream it," Rafael said.

Saint Michael stood, lifting the medallion. "So he remembers."

Jo wasn't certain what to make of that. Instead, she said to Saint Michael, "Why didn't any of you intervene? After the demon killed Chip, I thought we were done for."

Michael smiled. "No, you didn't."

She thought for a moment. No, she hadn't. She'd whispered to herself for courage, and thought that the situation must not have been bad enough for the angels to help. "I didn't believe he could harm me."

"*You* had faith," Assumpta said quietly.

Jo nodded. She'd had faith. But had it been faith in herself or faith in *them*?

Saint Michael nodded. "You didn't need us," he said. "But I need to take care of this." He hefted the medallion. He turned to the other angels and nodded.

Gabriel lifted his horn and blew. In a flash of light, all the angels were gone.

CHAPTER 38

SECONDS AFTER THE ANGELS LEFT, THE BELL OVER the front door of the shop rang, and Pournelle walked back in. He looked on, his face impassive. Jo tried to decipher what he might be thinking. But she had no idea—she couldn't get a read on him. He appeared thoughtful, but maybe not in a good way. He watched Assumpta care for Father Tony, but remained in the background, silent. He didn't offer to help—but maybe he didn't because he knew Father Tony, if conscious, would refuse.

Or, maybe he thought his skills weren't up to the task. Probably, he'd looked in from the outside, and seen the angels take care of the fallen priest.

Either way, she'd bet Father Tony would rather *die* before accepting assistance from Pournelle—which seemed rather foolish. But then, she'd witnessed a lot of good people do foolish things in the name of religion. Did they find a place in Heaven?

Jo shook her head to clear out that thought. *Not. Her. Problem.*

She took a deep breath, realizing her nausea had passed—which was a good thing. She had a lot of work ahead of her.

She looked around the store, taking in the blood-splashed walls; the bits of demon flesh littering the floor, the shelves and the ceiling. Merchandise was strewn about as though a fierce wind had made its way through the shop. She picked up the dented cauldron she'd hit Father Tony with, shaking out pieces of Chip which had made its way inside. Carefully, she set it on the counter. She felt depleted, listless, as she dusted off a stool. All the adrenalin-infused energy she'd had a short time ago had eroded in one fell swoop, leaving her exhausted.

Despite the fatigue, she felt good—better in a way she couldn't put her finger on. She wasn't going to die. That must be the explanation: a simple lightness of spirit. Relief.

Smiling, Jo looked down at the scarab—the beautiful copper and blue pendant rested warmly against her chest. She lifted the chain over her head and walked to Pournelle, holding it out to him. "It looks like I don't need this anymore."

"It wasn't a loan," he said, turning away from Assumpta and Father Tony. He brushed imaginary lint from his sleeve, then gave her his full attention.

"But the spell has been broken—I no longer have need of it."

"One can never have too much protection."

True. But she didn't know what to say to that, so she simply nodded—a quick bob of her head—and an awkward silence grew between them. She didn't know how they stood. The medallion still loomed between them—she'd known about it and never told him. Assumpta had never loaned it to her. Did Pournelle trust that she'd never used it against him? Were *they* okay? Finally, she asked, "What now?"

"'What now?'" He gave her a puzzled look.

"Yeah—*what now?* What's next for you?" She looked around the store, mentally calculating how much time it was going to take to clean up, and decided she'd rather get it all done this evening than go to bed and face it in the morning. "I've got hours of clean-up ahead of me, and then warding the place—which I was hoping Father Tony would help me with... So, there's even more for me to do here before sun-up. Good thing I'm feeling better." She smiled—tentatively—then paused. Pournelle was staring at Assumpta again, and Jo knew he was still wrestling with the fact that Assumpta had never told him about the medallion. "What about you?"

Pournelle gave her his attention again, raised his hand and snapped his fingers. Instantly the shop was set to rights—right down to the strawberry incense smoldering in its usual place, and the samovar bubbling away on the counter. "That should take care of the hardest bit," he said. "And I'm certain there's a spell in the demon book to repel demons or other beasties. That might do for now."

Jo felt oddly sick for even considering using the book again tonight. "You can ward against your own kind?"

"Don't you? Locks on doors, bars on windows..."

He had a point. But it didn't seem right, using a spell from a demon book to ward against demons. If the spell were in the book, wouldn't there be an equally useful counter-spell in the same book? One that any demon with his own personal copy of said book could use to break the warding spell?

It wouldn't do. She'd ward the store her way—the *right* way, as far as she was concerned. If Assumpta didn't go to the hospital with Father Tony, maybe she'd stick around and help.

"I should be going now," Pournelle said.

"Wait—" Jo lifted a hand.

The door slammed open with a rattle, the bell jangling disharmoniously and two paramedics rushed in, carrying a gurney. They fell to work beside Father Tony, asking Assumpta about all the blood on his robes, but no obvious wounds.

"Divine intervention," she answered. The paramedic looked at her disbelievingly, but Assumpta didn't elaborate. They couldn't rouse him, which seemed the more important issue.

Assumpta's cell phone rang. She looked down at the number and answered. "Hello?" A few seconds later she smiled. It didn't take a genius to know what was said. She disconnected and looked at Jo. "Sheila's okay."

"I'm glad," Jo said.

The paramedics belted Father Tony to the gurney and raised it. They rushed to the front door and got him into the ambulance.

"I'm going with him," Assumpta shouted over her shoulder, running after them.

When the door slammed behind her, the awkward silence between Jo and Pournelle grew.

Pournelle cleared his throat. "Well—I guess I'd better be going."

"Wait." Jo ducked behind the counter and retrieved the demon book. "Take this."

And there was that hopeful look on Pournelle's face again—the one she'd seen a few times before when he'd been around the book. Jo walked around the front of the counter, carrying the book in both hands; she held it out to Pournelle. "Witch to demon, I bestow this gift. May it always be where you think you've left it."

A smile, pure sunshine, lit Pournelle's face. He took the book with a reverence she didn't think him capable of. And when it was finally in his hands, he traced the gilded letters of the of the cover with his index finger, circling the ruby gem once, then again. "If it's not too much trouble..." He looked at Jo expectantly.

"Yes?"

"May I have the glasses, too?"

"Giving you the book doesn't allow you to read it?"

"Alas, no."

"Well, of course, then."

Even giving him the book didn't allow him to read it? Why not? He was a demon, after all—he already had the sight. She'd have to ask him about that someday—but not now. It didn't seem right to ruin his moment by questioning his abilities. She walked behind the counter and grabbed the glasses. She handed them over to him in their little coffin case, and then wondered if she'd done that wrong. But she didn't remember there being any ceremony about the glasses.

"Thank you," he said, pocketing them in his left breast pocket. Then he snapped his fingers, and he was gone, leaving Jo standing there all alone—quite bemused.

"Well, I do have work to do," she said, snapping on the radio. She poured a cup of tea, started collecting the things she needed to ward the shop, and got to work.